MICHELE MINER has been a professional freelance Production Stage Manager at theatres around the country, including the Mark Taper Forum and Geffen Playhouse in Los Angeles. She has stage managed both on and off Broadway and in Japan and Canada and she is a proud member of Actors Equity Association. She spent six years as the Production Manager in the Department of Theatre and Dance at Pomona College in Claremont, CA. She has also taught Stage Management at Pomona College. She is the mother of Giacomo and Justine and is married to Paul Perri, an actor, and teacher at AMDA.

THEIR MOON WAS CARDBOARD

A Matthey Cole Mystery

Michele
Miner

Printed in the United States of America.
(ebook)
(paperback)
ISBN 9781548865801

This book may be purchased at Amazon.com

First Edition: August 3-18

For Susie Walsh - colleague, friend, and accomplice.
And for all Stage Managers.

CONTENTS

THEIR MOON WAS CARDBOARD....

Chapter One

Jesus in a tortilla! "What does Jesus in a tortilla look like? His whole body on the cross?...or just his face? What do you say to your neighbour...call over the fence, 'Alma, come here. I'm fixing Rudy another taco and I start to throw the tortilla into the pan, I look down and--oh, my God--there's Jesus staring back at me, stigmata, the whole works. Christ, Alma, I could've fried the Son of God. Oye! It's a miracle!'"

Matthey Cole stared at the picture of the round, flat pancake. She tried to feel that her soul was being affected. That at any moment she would be struck by lightning, fall to her knees and see the truth. Instead she wondered what happens when 'Jesus in a tortilla' starts getting moldy and people still come from hundreds of miles away to look at it and kiss it and be healed? Jesus, what if they are healed?

Matthey put the *Time* magazine down and resumed eating her bowl of Product 19. It was Monday, her day off. She'd already done her 15 minutes of leg exercises. She'd completed her monthly struggle through of the "Maple Leaf Rag" on the piano. It was her attempt at family tradition. The "Maple Leaf Rag" was the only song her grandmother could play, and Scott Joplin's tune had been constantly pounded out on the keys at twice its recommended tempo throughout Matthey's visits. Her mother, who plays by ear, picked it up instantly and plays it even faster. Matthey took lessons for six years and is determined to eventually play the damn tune from memory either before she dies or before she has a daughter, whichever comes first. The way it was looking she had plenty of time to keep practicing.

The landline rang. She ignored it and kept eating. The answer machine picked up after five rings. She listened to her uninspired message with the perfunctory beep followed by "Hi, it's Bill. I just got in. The show went well. I'm going to sleep and then I have to get to 'StarFind' at 4:00. I'll call you late tonight or tomorrow." Click. Although she had a cell phone, she hated using it to receive calls unless she had to. Too easy to get in contact with her. Matthey always used a landline whenever possible. And the theater where she worked was all concrete, so her phone didn't work inside, anyway. Matthey regularly transferred her calls to various landlines. It was easy. And not many people had her cell number. Pretty much everyone she knew hated that about her.

Matthey looked at her two cats laying on the floor beneath her. "You know guys, Bill never says good-by. Just like characters on television. I've never understood that. Nobody hangs up the phone without saying so long or something. Well, I guess Bill does."

Matthey watched her fourteen-year-old, short-haired, black female cat jump up on the kitchen table and latch onto her little finger. "Hey, pal, don't suck my finger while I'm eating. OK, just for a minute." Gaffer's black and white brother, Cristo, jumped up on her lap, neatly covering the coffee stains that blended in with the greatly faded blue and purple swirls on the oversized Halley's Comet tee-shirt. "I know, sweetheart, but I can't pet you, eat my cereal and let

2

your sister chew on my little finger all at the same time. How come you guys aren't fat and lazing around in the sun all the time like cats are supposed to? OK, I'll make a deal here. You let me finish eating and then I'll lay on the couch and binge Netflix and pet you both all you want. Deal? OK. So, go run around for awhile. Go on. Beat it." Gaffer and Cristo both jumped down to the floor and sat looking up at her.

Lifting the cereal bowl to her mouth she downed the remaining milk. Her right eye spied the note she had tacked on her dartboard next to the NSA's phone number. *Inflexibility is never a valid defense against one's disappointments in life.* She had jotted this down the other night while talking on the phone to her favourite cousin in Tulsa. As they talked about his brother's lack of spouse, money and a steady job, it occurred to her that Sam, the oldest in that family, could only justify his own choices in life if he negated everyone else's. Or at least those that might have held an attraction for him, if he didn't have four kids and two mortgages. Matthey was determined to never be so rigid.

The phone rang again. Both cats looked over. "That's OK, guys, machine's still on. I can call them all back after a few episodes. Let's just turn the TV on." She plodded into the living room. After using three clickers and screwing up twice she got the Netflix logo.

"OK. Pause. Time for a tequila sunrise." Matthey headed back to the kitchen. Cristo followed her, meowing. "What are you talking about? Of course, it's not too early. It's almost noon. That's right, hack up that furball." She began opening cabinet doors. "A little tequila, a little orange juice and, oh, let's throw in five maraschino cherries this time. Mmmm. Beats brewers yeast. Yes, doll, I heard the message. I'll call Roger back later. He knows I don't answer phones Monday mornings. You'd think he'd learn by now.

Anyway, what the hell could he want, I just left him four hours ago. Oh, God, guys, I haven't fed you! Why didn't you say something? Alright, you did. Blend this baby, and then a bit of Purina."

Matthey checked the refrigerator for an open can of cat food and, finding none, looked in the cabinet above. "OK, guys, let's talk. Your dad thinks we should get back together, get some counseling and have a kid. I assume that means remarriage. What do you think? It might be acceptable. I ain't exactly gettin' any younger, you know. I mean I'm the only one that knows that playing the "Maple Leaf Rag" is an established tradition in our family. My mother would laugh and tell me, 'what a silly idea, there's no tradition like that. Honey, you have such lovely hair.' But my daughter would understand this legacy." She began spooning the new cat food into their individual bowls. "And Roger's basically a good man. I mean, we're really good friends. Even his adolescent, Twilight-loving bride calls me for advice, heh, heh. I tell her she's not understanding the subtext in her Zumba workout. Yeah, she doesn't find it too funny, either." She put the bowls down on the floor and washed off the spoon and opener. "And he'll be a good father, right guys? Listen, being allergic to you, and just about a million other things, doesn't count. He's not allergic to babies--of course, I always thought he was allergic to me. And he's trying so hard to be supportive and helpful. Maybe the counseling would help me want to sleep with him....

Matthey picked up her drink, threw in three ice cubes and went back into the living room and switched back to TV to a soap she had occasionally watched since childhood, and hoped that Jill would be killed once and for all this time. Matthey had worked with the actress once, on a very mediocre play, and felt her talents as an actor were only exceeded by her lack of talents as a human being. As she settled into the plaid, overstuffed armchair, she remembered that she had scheduled a prop meeting at 9:00 tomorrow morning. Picking up an old list and her notes off the bamboo coffee table she started to pencil in an updated prop list while she listened to Jill's pleas for mercy.

"We don't need the kazoo. Scratch that off. The jewelry scene is cut so we won't need any of the picnic stuff. El historiosa! Guess that means we'll need to double the suitcase. Oh, and her jacket. Right! Need to call Laurie at the costume shop. If I can finish this list before 2:00 I can run over to Bill's and print it and be back before rush hour. The view from this house is wonderful but it's sure more of a pain to run over to Sherman Oaks from Mt. Washington than it was from Hollywood. Have to get a new printer! The cats nuzzled into the crook of Matthey's left arm. Cristo kept trying to play with the pencil.

"Shouldn't you guys be washing yourself after eating? OK, three months in this place and your Mom should reach a few conclusions, right? Roger and baby and sneezing and coupon cutting, or Bill and, probably, no baby, a lot of mental abuse, an ulcer or two, and a lot of 'rising above it'. Doesn't seem like much of a choice, eh?" Matthey gave up trying to write and reached for her drink. Her right hand stroked the backs of the two cats.

"But, hey, Bill has his good points. Hell, I thought he was perfect at first, I was weak in the knees, no appetite, in love with him. Two years sure makes a difference. Perfect at making me miserable. Wake up Matthey. Dear Abby can make mincemeat of you." She dug a cherry from the bottom of the glass and popped it into her mouth. "But he's got a printer and a great dog! He's probably sleeping with his dog. Hell, at least he'd be sleeping with someone."

She looked down at the two purring cats. "OK, guys, this is your time but end of this episode I have to finish this prop list.

Matthey lay back in the armchair and petted and was suckled and sipped and wondered how Carl could possibly be such a bigoted and dumb cop not to know who had kidnapped Jill. And only Gaffer and Cristo were aware of the shadow that slipped out of the back bedroom and down the hall and, effortlessly, disappeared over the back-porch wall.

Chapter Two

As Dr. Tom jumped the eight-foot distance from the top of the porch to the ground below he envisioned how graceful he must look. His pudgy body had its legs tucked back and under; the head was down, protected; the back rounded, ready to accept the shock of landing; and the mind visualizing the athletic picture he was presenting to anyone watching. Of course, no one was.

His feet hit the ground between the azalea bushes, and as he began a forward roll, his mind already imagining the nimble steps he would take as he bounded to his car in the street below, Dr. Tom raised his head. In the fraction of a second available to him, he grasped the fact that his pathway was blocked by one of the most intricate webs ever seen. A web that would have awed Frank Lloyd Wright. A web with four bedrooms, five baths, a sundeck and a pool. A web whose living room was occupied by its exceedingly large, pregnant, red, furry and very panicked owner.

An instant after the arachnid heard and felt the crash of bushes separating, she found herself staring into two dark, cavernous, snorting holes filled with hairs dripping with perspiration and snot. She froze.

As Dr. Tom tried to stop his forward motion, he instinctively opened his mouth to scream which allowed his lips to easily encircle the golf ball sized, agitated spider. His face smashed through the centerfold of this month's *Better Webs and Gardens*.

The spider struggled frantically to retreat from the large, yellow stalactites and stalagmites that had grazed her fat body when she entered this horrible cavity. Dr. Tom tried, just as frantically, not to breath in and, instead, began vomiting up every bit of the strawberry ice cream and English muffins he had eaten two hours ago. The eight-legged mother-to-be, carried out of her hellhole by the first upheaval, scurried under the first leaf that her swell landed on and spent the next four weeks living in paper bags and twitching.

Dr. Tom scrambled deliriously away from vomit and hairy monsters, and clawing at the sticky, silky strands of webbing on his face, forgot his attempts at incognito. He ran around the house to the front door and started pounding on it.

Matthey opened her front door and discovered her therapist tearing at his throat and face, yelling about radiation and mutants. Vomit covered his clothes. For just a fraction of a second it reminded her of the Haagen Daas strawberry ice cream in her freezer.

"Dr. Tom, come in. Cup of coffee? Lysol? No, really, are you alright?"

Dr. Tom pushed past her and ran for the bathroom, stripping off his shirt as he went. Tearing open the window over the sink he threw the rest of his clothes out and jumped in the shower, soaking water into every pore until his pulse slowed and he became reassured that no multi-legged demons were lurking anywhere on his body. Stepping out of the tub he carefully shook out the towel before drying himself. After checking the pockets and turning the sleeves inside out he put on the faded purple, corduroy Montgomery Ward floor length bathrobe that was hanging on the back of the door. Sucking in his gut, he tightened the sash and went out to find Matthey. He only screamed once when Gaffer's black tail feathered past his ankle as he turned into the kitchen.

While Dr. Tom was showering, Matthey went out to the backyard. Finding his clothes, she carefully picked them up, using her garden gloves, and threw them in a trash bag which she put

8

alongside the driveway. She noticed the vomit covering the grass and the azalea bushes. She made a mental note to check her freezer.

Back inside she decided against coffee and instead handed Dr. Tom a tequila sunrise when he entered the kitchen. He successfully fought back another urge to upchuck at the sight of the dark round cherry lying at the bottom of the tall glass filled with red liquid. Closing his eyes, he drank the alcohol gratefully.

"So, Dr. Tom." Matthey leaned back against the counter. "Perhaps you can explain why you've decided to pay me a visit and perform your early morning toiletries at my house. I have the feeling you're not here to borrow a cup of sugar."

"You didn't come home last night!" Dr. Tom blurted out, not fully recovered. "Who were you with? I know it wasn't Bill or Roger. I know about them all. You've told me about them all. Your 'zap contentment' injunction will always get in the way. You'll never be happy."

"Tom, where I was last night is none of your business!"

"What do you mean, of course it's my business. You sit on my couch and make the most intimate details of your life my business."

"It's your business for one hour a week. An hour for which I now pay you fifty dollars. The remaining one hundred and sixty-five hours of the week are no concern of yours!"

"One hundred sixty-seven," Dr. Tom replied smugly.

"Your 'zap childish' injunction is showing, Tom!"

"It's only showing because I choose to make use of it at this time. One's injunction is always available and accessible. I just teach that one doesn't have to resort to it instinctively. One can choose when to use it."

"And I've just learned that I can choose to throw you and your pop psychology out with the cat litter."

9

"That just proves your 'zap contentment' won't allow you to accept my wisdom and avail yourself of knowledge that will bring you inner satisfaction. You're simply illustrating the very problem that I'm trying to enlighten you about. I love it when my theories are proven again and again."

"Why don't you explain my theory of why you're standing in my kitchen in my bathrobe! You were in my house last night!"

Dr. Tom decided aggressive honesty would be in her best interest. And possibly his. "Not all night. I followed you from the theatre to the Inside Passage Tavern, but I lost you when you left your ATM machine at 12:03am. I came here, cleverly eluded your neighbours and slipped in the bathroom window. You should do something about that. I know you didn't go to Bill or Roger's because they both called last night."

Matthey was momentarily caught off guard. "There were no messages on the machine when I got home."

"That's because I erased them. They both just wanted you to call and help them with errands or some nonsense. It's time you realized--"

"Dr. Tom," Matthey interrupted somewhat urgently, "were there any other messages?"

"Oh, your director called wanting to talk about Tuesday's rehearsal schedule. And some woman called, long distance, I think. She just wanted to know if you'd found out anything yet. Doesn't anyone you know sleep? And do you really expect guests to sleep comfortably on just a box spring on the floor?" And why don't they call your cell phone?"

"Hmmm, probably just an actor." Matthey glanced at the clock. "So, Dr. Tom, you still haven't explained your presence here. Not to mention sneaking into my house. It feels a bit creepy, you know. And that room is just storage. The box spring isn't for guests, invited or not."

The five foot-six, overweight, forty-two-year old shrink held out his glass for a refill. "I asked you, last visit, to call my answer machine every night and tell me about each moment of anxiety you've had that day and tell me what your ideal mother would have praised you for, and you haven't called once. I consider that evidence of repression and my therapy cannot stand still for that. I had to see what activities were causing you such shame that you had to hide them from your mother and me."

"And?" Matthey poured him more alcohol.

Dr. Tom let out a sigh. "And I was rejected again last night. She was beautiful. A court reporter. We were at the Pavilion watching <u>Figaro</u> and she excused herself at intermission complaining of something or other, her diabetes, I think, and she never came back to her seat. So, the next intermission, I left, and saw you getting into your car. And I decided I should allow my injunction to ease my despair by throwing myself into my work. Again, it was my choice. I didn't have to feel rejected and I didn't have to try to forget it by tailing you. I <u>chose</u> to!"

Matthey poured herself another drink. "Did it occur to you to ask someone to check on your friend in the restroom?"

"No, of course not. It was obvious that she found me unattractive and fat. I chose to be an adult and accept that fact, and not allow myself to consider more appealing alternatives like she had fallen into a diabetic coma. You see, I reach for my ideal mother buried inside me and I am comforted by the knowledge that she approves of my actions. Even if I were to find out three weeks from now that my date had died in the toilet while desperately trying to find the insulin that she had left in her other purse, I would still feel no guilt. I would know I had done what was right for me. My ideal mother had sanctioned it. Oh, Matthey, if you'd only commit yourself, you'd find those answers you're looking for.

Matthey pulled out three extra cherries from the jar. She enjoyed watching him flinch as she dropped them in her glass, one by one. "You're an amazing person, Dr. Tom. You and Los Angeles are well suited for one another. And it's more amazing that I actually agreed to start paying you."

Matthey had met Dr. Tom when she was stage managing for a theatre run by the American Legion. Several Iraq vets were among the cast. He had volunteered to come in each week and hold stress classes with the hope of alleviating some of the tension that was building up in the company. Part of his offer included ten free private sessions for each member of the company. He was writing a book and wanted the input. Matthey had eventually taken him up on his offer and had completed three sessions before quitting the Legion group. She felt obligated to complete the sessions and to start paying for the next visit and Dr. Tom didn't object. In fact, he took it as a sign that she now trusted him enough for him to confide in her.

She looked at her psychologist. His gut had relaxed into its more natural protruding position. "You're not unattractive or fat. You just may try too hard. Did you propose to this one, too?"

"No! I only asked if she was fertile. Wait, she didn't get upset. She said she supposed she was. Matthey, I'm forty-two. Every Sunday, seventeen brothers, uncles, nephews and cousins gather at my parents' house. Every Sunday I entertain them with stories about my patients and the theatre people I've met and every Sunday night I wave good-by as they leave with their children and their wives and get into their Volvos, and all I want to do is cry and eat coffee ice cream and have my father put his arms around me and tell me he's proud of me just the way I am, but I don't and he doesn't and we shake hands and I drive off alone with my Tupperware full of potato salad that no one ate. Matthey, I don't want much. Just a good looking wife, two bright kids, a thriving practice and my book published. Don't leave me, Matthey. I need to succeed with you, to make you whole. To show you how to make decisions. I need it for me and my father and--do you have any clothes I can borrow?"

"Uh, yeah, I'll dig up something." Matthey headed into her bedroom. "So, what happened, anyway?"

"Oh, the flu. Must be catching the flu. Hey, there was one other call, I think. I don't know. I was asleep when the phone rang. Might have just been a hang up but, it's funny, I'm just thinking of it now. I seem to remember some foreign accent and something that sounded like... 'chaga scone,'--or something. I forgot about it until just now. The mind's amazing, isn't it?"

Matthey was about to pull an old pair of oversized sweats off the closet shelf. Her arm hesitated for only a second.

Chapter Three

Matthey convinced Dr. Tom to leave twenty minutes later, promising him she would think about being at her next scheduled session. She also promised she'd get him tickets to her play, Amazon Loophole. She wondered why she didn't get him arrested instead.

It was now almost 2:00 in the afternoon. In Washington, D.C. it would be 5:00. If she hurried, she might catch Debbie on the phone before she left work. Taking the number off the dartboard she dialed it plus about 10 extensions. Hundreds of digits later she heard the click of a receiver being picked up at the National Security Agency.

"Uh, can I please speak to Debbie McNamara? Oh, yeah, I've got it here, 'decide...who...stays...up...and...who...goes...down...' Sure, I'll hold."

Debbie McNamara had been Matthey's first and best friend when the Cole family had moved to St. Louis during her kindergarten year. They became bonded together by a mutual love for animals, music and the "M" club--a top secret organization whose members had to have a name starting with an "M". There were three members. The third, Marilyn Invernett, was now living in Pakistan trying to organize women's softball. Debbie was the only person able to get Matthey to even look at a Barbie doll.

Then came junior high school with hundreds of new seventh graders from a dozen grade schools converging on Tellmon Junior High. Somehow Debbie's twelve-year-old instincts grasped the pecking order of cliques and popularity and she plunged in. Matthey was awed by the fact that at the end of the first week of school everyone knew who the most popular kids were. And everyone, including her, knew where he or she fit on the scale. She didn't remember any ballots being given out. And she knew her position wasn't as high as Debbie's.

So, Debbie and Matthey no longer played together but at the end of each school year Debbie would fill a page of Matthey's yearbook with reminiscences of how wonderful it used to be. With the exception of the odd birthday card they lost touch over the years. Three summers ago, Matthey was in St. Louis visiting her mother and decided enough time had gone by. She called Debbie and they had lunch. Debbie came in the restaurant looking just as short and cute as always. Her mid-calf length cloth coat made her appear motherly and middle class. She ordered a strawberry daiquiri and had only one. She had two kids, a boy and a girl, and her husband, whom she married out of college, was a junior executive in a bank. The Midwestern nasal twang still rang in her voice.

Debbie also had a Ph.D. in Spanish and Portuguese, spoke seven languages fluently, spent an hour every day practicing the piano, was working on her second Ph.D. in Spanish literature, worked as a freelance translator out of her home and had just started taking classes in Russian. And she didn't bring out pictures of her kids. Matthey decided she had obviously been an extraordinary child to be perceptive enough to pick Debbie for a best friend at the age of five.

As they ate lunch, they discovered that they had both called the CIA out of curiosity. The organization had been very interested in Debbie. Matthey admitted she'd smoked pot in college and her Spanish was limited to billboards. She received a generic form letter thanking her for her interest.

After this visit they kept in touch by letters, and four years ago Debbie and family moved to Washington, D.C. where she had accepted a job with the National Security Agency as a translator doing "top secret" stuff. Matthey hadn't spoken with her until a week ago.

The receiver in her hand emitted several clicks and beeps. "Matthey! I'm sorry to keep you waiting. I was on another line. One of the kids was telling me about her Halloween costume. Remember when we used to stay out for hours and bring back bagsful of candy.

So, how's Roger? Divorced yet? Any chance of your coming out here with Bill when he does the White House Christmas show?

"Debbie, aren't all these phone calls recorded?"

"Oh yes. We have rooms filled with tapes. Of course, now it's all digital."

"Well, then can we skip the personal stuff. Did you call me last night? A friend erased my machine, but he said a woman had called long distance."

"Yes, that was me. So, who's the friend?"

"Not important. He also thought someone had called with a foreign accent who left a message that sounded like 'chaga scone'. To someone asleep Che Gascon could sound like 'chaga scone'--"

"Who was asleep?"

"What do you think? Why would he be calling me? How'd he get my number? How does he even know my name?"

"Well, have you been talking to anybody?"

Debbie had called Matthey a week ago to enlist her help in a situation that she had become aware of through translating some correspondence that had been found in a small plane that crashed near the Texas border. The flight had originated from Panama, with stops in Carracas and Cozumel. The plane and the majority of its contents (legal and illegal) were being dissected and filed by the appropriate agencies but one letter found in the pocket of the pilot found its way to Debbie's desk. The letter was from Che Gascon and was addressed to his cousin, the pilot, Wanda Villanueva, in San Antonio. The letter spoke of his intention to come to Los Angeles and become an actor. He was working on his English, lifting weights and reading Shakespeare. He and his friend, Jacqueline, had made arrangements and would leave her hometown of Bucerias, Mexico in early September and planned to arrive in Los Angeles a few days later. If all had gone well, they should have been happily going out on auditions for over a month now.

Debbie's husband, Ben Gardner, had vacationed in Puerto Vallarto seventeen years ago. He and his fraternity friends had stayed at a house several kilometers north of the town. Almost every day they drove into the nearby village of Bucerias to buy bottled water and groceries. They had the house for a month. For the first week Ben joined his buddies for the nightly partying and boozing. But he soon wearied of the atmosphere that made him feel as if he had never left the frat house and he took to driving into Bucerias around twilight. There, he would get some helado and sit on a bench in the town square and listen to the villagers laugh and sing and play music and he felt very content and very much an outsider. Over time a young girl took notice of him and, eventually, things proceeded as they often do, and Ben flew home waving good-by to his virginity and the beginnings of a pregnancy.

The girl wrote to him that she had named her daughter, Jacqueline, after a relative of Ben. And Ben sent a money order to a Senora Lopez twice a year for as much as his conscience demanded. Nothing was ever asked of him. Now he had reason to believe his daughter was in southern California likely trying to become an actress and living with Che Gascon. Debbie, typical of most people living east of Los Angeles, assumed Matthey knew everybody in Hollywood and suggested to Ben that she ask her to look around. Ben didn't know what his daughter's last name would be. He didn't think it was Lopez. He also didn't know what he would do if Matthey found her. But he was aware of some of the contents in the plane and he did know that the final paragraph of the letter bragged about Che's "solid connections to some of the biggest names in the business" and how he was sure, by calling in a few debts, his rise to fame would be fairly

17

quick. Ben and Debbie thought the worst of Che and assumed he dealt in cocaine and other drugs.

Matthey's attention returned to the receiver in her hand. "Debbie, last night I went to a party in Malibu."

"Ooooh. Anyone famous?"

"Yes, lots. Anyway, I finally left around 7:00 in the morning. I don't know how these people do it. At least half of them had to be at work this morning. I must have been offered cocaine three dozen times. Seems to be the drug of choice again. I even gave Roger's wife a ride home. I mentioned Che's name to everyone. With no description it's a little hard. At any rate, no one showed any indication of recognizing him."

"Well, obviously, someone did. Someone who knew him well enough to contact him and give him your name. Did he leave a number?"

"I don't know. I don't think so, maybe, but it was erased."

"Well, he'll probably call back. Be careful. Isn't it exciting! Remember how the "M" club used to tail people after school? Remember spying on that guy in Mrs. Ash's house who exercised in the nude? Remember how you used to sneak aboard the trains while they were waiting at the station? You said, wear dark clothes and always look them in the eyes."

"Thanks, Debbie, I'll get out my trench coat immediately. I'll call if anything else happens. Someday, I'd really like to meet your family. Give them my love."

Matthey hung up, got her cell phone and inserted it in the speaker next to her and brought up her playlist. Bonnie Raitt's voice filled the room. She tried to remember who she talked with at the party.

Chapter Four

After her preview performance last night, she had gone out with some of the cast members to the local theatre bar, the Inside Passage. One of the actors mentioned that his agent was pushing him to attend a party at this big producer's house who lived at the beach in Malibu. Said it would help his career. Jason, the actor, had arrived in

Los Angeles from Iowa only six months ago and would have preferred to spend all his time at home working on his role in the play but he was afraid to cross his agent and he begged Matthey to go with him. Jason was only twenty-six, six foot two and very good looking. His agent was fifty-seven, very powerful and never married.

Seeing a chance to ask a few questions of "some of the biggest names in Hollywood" about their connections she surprised everyone by agreeing to go. She surprised herself more. They made arrangements for her to follow him in her car.

"I hope I'm not really doing this thinking I'm going to find Mr. Deus Ex Machina," she said to her rearview mirror. "Get serious, lady, you'd have more luck in the laundromat. Now, now, you never know. Someone there might be straight, available, intelligent, witty and shrink free. Maybe, but he'll still have a subscription to Variety and drink too much. Matthey, you're not exactly a teetotaler. Fine, but I'm not an alcoholic, either. Listen, Cole, if you want perfection, you're going to have to learn to squint a little."

Matthey stopped at her ATM machine to get enough money to buy gas at the cash only place next door. Jason didn't notice her stop and kept heading for the freeway. Some guy tried to follow her but when you're a single woman you get used to that often enough and she easily ditched him. She called Jason on his phone and he pulled over until she could catch up with him.

Other than the usual scanning looks as they entered each room of the two-story beach house it turned out to be a halfway decent party. It still amazed her that people could size you up so quickly and decide you weren't "somebody". She must have been daydreaming in seventh grade when you learned this stuff. Matthey had once thrown Jon Voight out of an actor's dressing room after the half hour call because she didn't recognize him. One more thing to blame her mother for not teaching her. Along with never figuring out hair rollers or how to make a kitchen floor look clean and shiny. Guiltily, she left Jason in the hammerlock grip of his agent and started mingling.

As she sipped on Bushmills and munched on fresh crab meat she tried to join in every conversation she encountered. Since the majority of them were the same conversation it was relatively easy to toss in a tidbit she had just picked up and quickly endear herself as just another broad looking to make a buck and show these sons of the network bitches who'd turned down her last project. Two years with Bill had taught her a few things. Whenever she could she'd drop Che's name and ask if anyone knew him or how to get in touch with him. No one seemed the least interested in her questions and everyone appeared genuine in their lack of knowledge. She did get several names of dealers, all offered eagerly and with a sense of pride. Three were junior execs in the "Biz", one was a female co-host on a quiz show, and one was an ex-child star who never grew above four feet three inches.

Somewhere between the pool and the beach Matthey ran into Denise, Roger's presumably soon to be ex-wife. Except no one had told her. Denise was a production assistant on "Love Snuggle", a contestant show that was receiving a cult following across the country. She was enormously proud to be associated with the show.

"Matthey! Whatever are you doing here? I love your boots. Roger's not here. The old wuss wanted to get some sleep. He's doing some carpentry work for Barney, over there by the sushi, tomorrow, that I got him, and he said he always feels so out of place at these parties, that he hates TV people. You'd think he'd be so proud of me that I got this fabulous job on my very first interview."

Roger was also a stage manager in theatre but didn't work often enough to support a household and he had recently started working freelance as a carpenter. Matthey knew he would have killed their un-conceived child to be in TV.

"I'm sure he is very proud of you, Denise."

"Did you read in *People* Magazine where we have the highest daytime rating of any game show in the two o'clock slot, ever? I just adore Jerry. He's so cool and he picks his wardrobe himself."

Jerry was the "Love Snuggle" host. He signed off each day by slapping himself in the forehead and shouting, "Don't <u>you</u> forget to snuggle with the one you love!" He had thought this tag up himself and now nerds across America emulated him.

"Matthey, can I catch a ride home with you later? I rode in with two of the girls from work. We were at the RM#fing concert. They can drive me home but they both live on the west side and now you're only a mile from us. Nobody lives on that side of town."

Matthey cancelled any hope of a sexually depraved encounter with some sensitive soul seeking respite from the shallowness of Tinseltown and agreed to find Denise when she was ready to leave. Walking on alone to the beach she lay down in the sand and gazed up at a glorious star filled sky with a waning moon. And immediately fell asleep. Three hours later she woke up, discovered the party still in full swing, found Denise in the kitchen and headed home.

They arrived at Roger's house as the third Sig Alert was being announced during the morning's rush hour. They had been driving for two hours. Denise had stayed awake for the first five minutes. Denise insisted that she come in and at least have a cup of coffee and say hello to that old grouchy wouchy while she showered and changed for work.

"Hi, honey, we're home," Matthey called out. Denise giggled and headed for the bathroom.

She went into the kitchen and found a fairly fresh pot of coffee. Picking up a mauve mug with hippos encircling it she poured herself a cup of coffee. She was adding milk when Roger came in from outside, holding a cordless drill.

"Still can't bear to kill aphids with your hands, eh?"

"Honey, what the hell are you doing here?" Roger rushed over to hug her and Matthey raised her hot mug up in the air trying to keep it from spilling. "Let's get pregnant. Let me kiss your buns. I won't mind working on other people's houses if it's for us, my kids. I want to turn on Sesame Street for my child, not my wife. God, you're beautiful!"

Matthey extricated herself and sat down at the table. "Roger, can it! She'll hear you. I'm only here because I met Denise at this party and gave her a ride home. She seems quite happy here with you."

"She's in the shower. She doesn't hear anything she doesn't want to. She's only happy because she's always gone. At parties or at clubs or at work mooning over old hairy Mr. Snuggles. Of course, she's happy. This is a free place to rinse out her twenty-five-dollar socks." Roger put his drill down on the table.

"Matthey, I love you. You are an adult, I'm an adult. I have to leave her. Help me. I'll take allergy shots, we'll get a maid, you can even talk to me while the sports are on. I don't clip coupons anymore."

"Stop pressuring me. I said I wanted some time. Your decision about Denise has to be completely independent from my decision about you. Roger, I'm tempted, I actually am, god knows why, but I don't want to make the same mistakes all over again.

There's got to be more to us together than just having a baby, I hope. So, how are you doing, anyway. How's your father holding up? You look tired."

"I am! All I do is sleep. He's doing alright, you know Big Frank. Still cracking dirty jokes. Why were you at that party? You hate those things."

"It wasn't so bad. Listen, if you ever hear the name Che Gascon mentioned in any connection will you let me know. Actor, drug dealer, anything."

"Why do you want to find a drug dealer. If it's your director, you can get valium anywhere. Tell him to chill out."

"No, just trying to do a favor for a friend. I don't want any drugs, just Che."

Denise came out of the shower wrapped in a mint green hapi coat and fixed a brewer's yeast and yogurt concoction. She turned up the radio, gushing over the new rock group, the Moody Blues. Trying not to listen to the two of them bickering, Matthey put her coffee mug in the sink and made excuses to leave.

Two and a half miles later, back in her wonderful little, quiet house on the side of a hill on Mt. Washington, and she punched in Bonnie Raitt and read the headlines on the front page of the L.A. Times. As Bonnie Raitt started the first notes of "Guilty" Matthey tried so hard to remember something of consequence that she fell sound asleep. Gaffer and Cristo arranged themselves around Matthey's knees and chest and joined her in slumber. Her cell had been dead for hours but calls automatically transferred to the landline. That phone awoke them, and Dr. Tom, about three hours later. It was a wrong number.

Chapter Five

Matthey entered the stage door of the Parkinson Hopkins Theatre at 8:45am on Tuesday. Waiting for her in the stage manager's office was the assistant stage manager, Tony Nieters, and the production assistant, Carole McDonald. Tony was in his early forties, married to a stuntman and had worked several shows with Matthey.

He grinned at her as she dumped her purse and canvas bag on the desk.

"Well, good morning! Talked to Jason yesterday. He couldn't get through to you on the phone. Seemed like everyone called me about rewrites. Jason said you had quite a time at the party. Said there were a bunch of guys wanting to know who you were. I tried calling last night but your line was always busy. So, did we have a good day off?"

"The cats knocked the phone off the hook, and I had a very pleasant time by myself, thank you!"

"Matthey, would you like me to get you a cup of coffee?" Though over 30 years old Carole was a recent graduate of the University of Arizona and had never before worked in professional theatre.

"Thanks, Carole. I can get it myself. Listen, I didn't have the time to type anything up so just work off your notes, OK? And let's make sure Joe writes everything down. I'm tired of hearing him always say that no one told him."

Joe McRacken was the assistant set designer and the person primarily responsible for obtaining the props. Most good-sized, professional theatres employed a prop person whose sole purpose was to acquire the chairs, tables, wine glasses, etc. that were used in any play on the stage. But the Hopkins tried to save money by making it part of the job of the assistant to the designer of the set. Most assistants begrudged this additional task. On Monday, Joe had been out of town attending a family funeral.

After Sunday's preview performance, the director, Alan Previn, had decided to cut one of the scenes. This change in the script instigated several rewrites. The meeting this morning was to relay any notes that would require new props, or changes in existing ones, to Joe so he would have them ready for the afternoon rehearsal. It was also a chance for the two stage managers and Carole to plot out changes in prop presets and running order. Matthey, as production stage manager, would also need to use the time to plot any changes in lighting, sound and costumes. She wished she hadn't slept through Monday.

The play, Amazon Loophole, was a world premiere. It had been written by a new playwright, Roman Malon, who had spent seventeen of his fifty-seven years living in Brazil as a saxophone player who also ran a small commuter airline. The story centered around the crusty, old, French, coffee plantation owner; his educated but suspiciously mysterious, yet sexy foreman, who is also his nephew; and a young girl who arrives on their doorstep after fleeing her mountain village because of famine and disease. Among many other themes, Malon was trying to suggest that innocence and simplicity are, inherently, greater powers than greed and solid business sense. Because the script called for the girl to be naked throughout most of the play several people had walked out of the two previews that had already taken place. There had been several phone calls complaining about the "pornography" and threatening to cancel subscriptions.

The majority of the rewrites were to be an attempt to modify the nudity without comprising the integrity. Tony had pointed out that this problem had already been faced, successfully, by owners of Kit Kat clubs across the city. Alan hadn't been amused. He planned to go places with his Hopkins directing credit.

From 1:00pm until 6:00pm the actors would rehearse the script revisions and all other performance notes onstage. The crew would also be involved in this rehearsal and all the technical elements would be available. Matthey would sit in the house on headset orchestrating the sound and light cues. Tony would be backstage supervising props and costumes. Carole would be on book, feeding actors their lines, if called for. The actors wouldn't arrive for another three and a half hours.

By 10:00am Joe was reluctantly on his way to acquire still more genuine Brazilian artifacts. Tony and Carole went across the street to the offices to find the playwright and his rewrites, and xerox, collate and date the new pages. Matthey tried to concentrate on her light cues. The designer was coming at noon to get her notes. The phone rang again immediately.

"Backstage. Hi. Nancy. Yes, no problem, I'll figure out the shots this afternoon. Is the photo call at 3:00 or 3:30 tomorrow? Great. Yeah, I'll make sure he calls you about his bio. Right. Bye." The phone rang immediately.

"Backstage. Don. Hi. Yeah, Joe's left. No, he said he'd be back at the shop by eleven-thirty. I told him to go to the County Fair this afternoon. They have lots of booths dealing in Amazon goods. Remember, I worked it last year selling Russian music makers? Don't worry, he said he'd notify you of any purchase over fifty dollars before he buys anything. Yeah, I'll tell him. Bye."

"Backstage. Laurie. Yes, I called to let you know you're going to have to double Mrs. DuValier's jacket. Yeah, we've cut the jewelry scene so there's no time to switch it. Well, if we can get it by 3:00pm it should be OK. I'm sure we'll rehearse the first act cuts first. Yeah, sorry. Really! When's the party? Well, if the photo call tomorrow ends early enough, I'll try to get to the shop. If I can't, tell her I'll miss her, OK? Oh, and tell her congratulations on the baby. See you later."

"Backstage. Bill! Hi, darlin'. Oh, nothing much, we're putting in a few cuts and I'm just trying to plot out a few things. You did? One of the cats knocked over the phone and I didn't realize it till this morning. Cell was dead. I'm sorry I missed your call. It would have been nice to see you. What did you do last night? No, I didn't get a chance to turn the TV on. Oh, you know, working on the script and things. I went to a party the night before and got in kind of late so I was pretty tired--sure I can come over tonight. It might be pretty late. The show comes down at ten, but we'll have notes after. Will you still be awake? No, really, if you're going to be asleep then I should skip it. Well, why don't you just call backstage around nine and let me know. OK, I'll call you then, when I'm done. Well, don't let the machine answer. Pick up the phone when you hear me. Bill, there's no point in coming over if you're sound asleep. What's the matter, bad day, already? Poor baby. Oh, I'm sure he's not really angry. Probably just had his feelings hurt by not being your first choice. Well, maybe he does understand. Maybe he's just upset about the deal on the house falling through. Well, just a thought. OK. I'll come by after. It'll be late though. OK. Yeah, me too. See you later."

Matthey hung up the phone and looked at herself in the wall mirror in front of her desk. A dark, thick mop of long hair looked back at her. Pushing her hair back from her face she gazed unselfconsciously at her image, evaluating herself mostly through the comments of others. Blue, deep set eyes. Widow's peak. Clear skin. Full lips. A hated bump in the nose. The kind of face that people found pretty at first meeting but that caused men to eventually exclaim about her beauty after knowing her awhile. Matthey feared she looked like Polly Bergen or worse, a generic straight A high school cheerleader, but she recognized that she exuded something that encouraged men to treat her in a very un-cheerleader fashion.

Sometimes with utmost respect and other times with a coat over their crotch. Usually both at the same time. It wasn't unsatisfying.

Matthey went out to the kitchen area to get another cup of coffee. Jay, the union prop man, had just finished making a fresh pot.

"Hey, finally going to be sociable. I come in, I give you a nice 'good morning, Matthey. Would you like a doughnut' and I get this little flutter from the back of your hand."

"Jay, I was on the phone. Good morning. No thanks, I don't want a doughnut but thank you for offering. We've cut the jewelry scene. Tony will give you the changes. We'll need to be set up from the top of Act I." Impatient at waiting for the pot to fill up she pulled it from under the machine and held her mug underneath the slow stream of coffee.

Jay sighed. "Yes, thank you for asking. I had a wonderful day off. I drove up to Big Bear. Took the convertible. Want to see the prints?" Jay reached into his shirt pocket.

"Prints, really?"

"Polaroids. See, if you lay these five end-to-end, they make one panorama view of the sunset from the north end of the lake. Beautiful, huh?"

"Yes, very pretty. You can kinda do that with an iPhone too you know? Yeah. So, you ever go out with Beth again?"

"Naw. I called her a few times, but she always said she was busy and to try her again. You ever talk to her?"

"No. Not since the time I brought her to the theatre. I really thought you guys would hit it off. You sure she's not interested. That she's not really busy? Isn't there some doubt in your mind? Before you just write it off?"

30

"Can't work that way. You give it an honest shot. You know if it's not working. You cut it loose. Can't go around what iffing all your life."

"How do you keep from doing that?"

"Get yourself a goal. Draw a straight line to it. Anything that's not on the line, get rid of it."

"What if nothing's ever on the line?"

"Change your goal."

"What if you don't have another goal. What if you're not sure what your goal should be in the first place?"

"You're what iffing too much. Your phone's ringing."

Matthey replaced the coffee pot and headed back to her office.

"Backstage. Oh, Alan. Fine. Yes, I've been here since 9:00am. Oh, my cell was dead. Yes, it's charged now. No, I haven't heard, what? Oh, Christ! Is she alright? Oh, my God! Oh, shit. When did it happen? Jesus! Uh, yeah, sure, I'll get a script to casting. Rehearsal still at 1:00pm? No, no, don't take more valium. There's a lot of work to do today. Yes, I'll make arrangements here. Bye."

Matthey sat at her desk twirling her templet with her pencil. Tony and Carole rushed in at the same time.

"Yeah, I know, I just heard."

"What happened? We only know that Christine had a car accident."

"She's dead!" They both gasped. "Late Sunday night, after the preview. She was driving home on the 710 and someone sideswiped her. She swerved into the guardrail, spun around and got smashed in the driver's side by a Trans Am that was behind her. She was killed instantly. The kids in the Trans Am are in intensive. They'll probably be alright. This guy in a pick-up going the other way thought the hit and run was maybe a Chrysler or Pontiac. You know,

31

mainstream, white, four-door family car. They haven't been able to talk to the Trans Am yet."

"Is the theatre going to do a memorial?" Tony started looking for his contact sheet.

"I don't know. I imagine. Maybe not. Listen, will you call the other actors? They should know before they get here."

"Already doing it."

"Thanks. Carole, put a set of the new pages into a clean script and run it over to casting. They've apparently known about this since yesterday. I want to call her boyfriend. Oh God, poor Jeci. He must be devastated."

Matthey had no idea what she was going to say to Jeci. She mainly knew him over the telephone. He'd been the only one home when she called to tell Christine she had gotten the job as understudy for the young Brazilian native. The role meant she could stop waitressing, get her Equity card and, hopefully, get an agent. Jeci had been so proud and excited Matthey had hung up in tears. His enthusiasm reminded her of the old Purina commercials. That one with the estranged but now reuniting father and son had always caused her to sob. So, did the ad showing the dog faithfully waiting by the farmhouse road for four years waiting for her owner to return from college. Matthey was an easy cry. Several calmer phone conversations with Jeci had followed and she eventually met Christine's now fiancé on the night of the first preview. He had been wearing a suit and tie, an anomaly in a Los Angeles audience. They had insisted she join them for a drink after notes.

Listening to the phone ring in her ear, she wished she hadn't liked them so much. And she wished she wasn't aware that she was already thinking about Christine's replacement.

Chapter Six

The <u>Amazon Loophole</u> company was onstage rehearsing the new shift between the piano scene and the porch scene. The jewelry scene used to come between these. For a reason known only to Alan, he had decided to start with the Act Two changes. Matthey, sitting by the tech table in row "L", was in the process of erasing the old sequence of light and sound cues from her script when George, the casting director, slithered into the seat next to her. She automatically shifted away from him, to her left--an instinctive gesture to avoid his foul breath and his obsequious manner.

George had once been an associate producer "back East" and had somehow convinced a few of the people around the Hopkins that he was competent in that field as well as casting. Unfortunately, it was the few that mattered.

George had a firm grasp of how to manage people using a variation of the Peter Principal. He only told people to do what he knew they would have done anyway, up to their level of incompetence. He could, very securely, inform directors, producers or whomever that "it was being taken care" because he knew "it" had already been crossed off a list by someone who had thought of "it" before George even knew "it" existed. If he was working with someone not so competent, his verbiage switched to "I'm sure it *will* be taken care of." Those taking "care of it", both competent and less so, all tried to ignore George whenever it was possible. It wasn't easy. His casting assistant, Myrna, came in to work at eight o'clock each morning and left around eight in the evening. George drifted in and out for, maybe, a total of four hours a day. He had a wonderful, guileful knack for, unassumingly, taking credit for Myrna's and everyone else's talents. Norman, the Hopkins' artistic director, thought he was invaluable and liked having him around. George liked Matthey.

"We've found someone fantastic to replace Christine!"

"Wonderful, I'll sign her name to the sympathy card."

"Call Myrna for the spelling. No, maybe you shouldn't do that. It might not look good."

"Right."

"I'm still negotiating with her manager. No agent. She'll be perfect. She's just turned eighteen and she's beautiful, you know what

I mean. Her English is very basic but, you know, with this part it doesn't matter." George shifted left. Matthey put her right foot up on her seat sitting like a standing Watusi warrior.

"Does she know about the nudity?"

"Her manager says it's not a problem. He'd die to get her into the Hopkins. This is his only client and he knows we want her so he's trying to get over minimum. For an understudy! Please! Face reality. He'll settle soon enough."

"Where's she from?"

"Some wonderful little town in Mexico, you know. You're going to adore her. Pick up a Spanish phrase book."

"Does she have her green card?"

"Well, of course. I'm sure Myrna's checked on that. They should be coming in tomorrow to sign the contract and I'll make sure she brings it with her."

"How'd you find her? What is her name, anyway?"

"Isabel Reyes. Uh, Myrna and I were at a 99 seat show last week and they--her and her manager, boyfriend, I think--came up to us at intermission. I was too tired to stay for the second act, but Myrna talked with them. Then I ran into them at a party a few nights later and we spent a long time talking about the play. When I heard the news yesterday, you know, I immediately thought of her. Spent quite a bit of time trying to track her down. The number they had given me was disconnected. I finally got hold of a mutual friend from the party and Che called me this morning."

"Che! Che who?"

"Che Gascon. Why, do you know him?"

"No! Uh, no. The name's just slightly familiar that's all."

"You're thinking of the pedophile character in the show we're doing up at the Lab."

"Yeah, probably am. When's Che coming in?"

"As soon as we get the money settled. Probably tomorrow morning. I gave him your number to call. He wants to know about rehearsal schedule."

"Uh, right. Well, thanks, George. Will you have Myrna call backstage with all the info on, what's her name?"

"Isabel."

"Yeah, Isabel. I'll have to call Equity. I assume she's non-Equity."

"Oh, I'm sure. Check with Myrna. Oh, there's Edward." George popped a mint into his mouth. "Listen, if anyone comes looking for me, tell them I'll be back in the office around four. Edward and I are going to have lunch somewhere. You'll take care of things, won't you? Oh, and sign my name to that card. You're a doll."

"Oh," Matthey called out. "And take care of those sniffles."

As she watched George go off with his arm around Edward, the head usher's shoulder, she flashed for Tony to get on headset backstage.

"What's up? You want me?"

"Yeah, will you call Myrna in casting and ask her for all information on Isabel. Can't remember her last name. She's supposed to take over the understudy job. Find out if she's Equity. Check if she has a green card. Don't want to get screwed on that one again. See if there's any phone number, address, whatever. Ask Myrna to send over a copy of the start form if they've done it yet. Oh, and tell her, as usual, George will be out of the office for awhile. Yeah, lunch with the new, blonde head usher. Probably needs another roommate to help with rent. Sorry! I know, that wasn't funny. I know! I'm sorry! Unforgiveable, yes, I know. Yeah, uh, thanks. No, no emergency, just call when you have a chance between cues. Bye."

"Way to go, Cole," Ronny, the sound man said over the headset.

"Just yesterday, Tony was talking about how hard it still was losing that room at George's" the master electrician, Charlie, chimed in.

"Obviously, a very tender subject with him," added Annie, the lighting designer.

"OK, OK, guys. Can we keep the headsets clear. I'm trying to listen to the rehearsal. We're doing cues here." Matthey's right leg ached from the bent position and she straightened it up, resting it on the seat in front of her.

She sat there, her mind mulling over all the questions. Was Isabel also Jacqueline? Probably. She couldn't possibly have a legal green card already. Does Che still want to be an actor? He must. He couldn't have become bitter and negative already. Why did he call her on Monday? Maybe he didn't. Maybe it was just some guy named Chuck Gascap,...Junior. "Hmmm, I'll have to talk to Dr. Tom and find out when he called?"

"Matthey, you're mumbling," Ronny spoke into her ear.

"Sorry, just thinking. OK, company, time for a break," Matthey called out. "Ten minutes!" She stumbled out of her aisle heading backstage. Alan bounded up the steps toward her.

"What do you think? I think the rewrites are brilliant. I think I've done a wonderful job of re-blocking them around the fireplace, don't you? Will you talk to Gloria? She's so upset about Christine. I'm afraid she's not going to be on top of it tonight. She's still got a ways to go and this is no time to be slacking off. And with the Shubert guy coming from New York on Friday, I'm worried. She's got to be up, optimistic, sweet. Gloria's moping around like her best friend's been killed. Talk to her."

"Why don't you take a valium, Alan. I'm sure she'll be fine tonight. It can be hard having your understudy killed by a hit and run. I'm sure you understand. It'll take her a little time, but she'll be alright. Did you know they figured out that they have, had a second cousin in common?"

"Really. Poor girl. I saw George here. Have we signed that girl Myrna told me about?"

"Do you know her? Have you met her?"

"No, I just told George that if he thought she was perfect that was good enough for me."

Matthey sighed. "We should be signing her tomorrow, apparently."

"Great. Do you think Carole could get me a cup of coffee? One sugar, no milk. I'll be with Annie. I'm not sure that last cue is the mood I want. You think? How many more minutes do we have?"

Matthey looked at her watch. Guessing, she said "now, only five, thanks." As she ran backstage, she almost tripped over Carole who was carefully replacing the spike marks with new tape.

"Carole, you don't have to do that. The old marks are fine. Oh, Alan asked if you'd get him coffee. He's sitting up with Annie.

Carole went scurrying for the coffee pot and Matthey headed for her office. She stopped short, seeing that Gloria was using the phone. She stood there trying not to look impatient while Gloria sat on the couch, speaking quietly into the receiver. Even though cell coverage was bad in the theatre because of all the concrete, actors were not allowed to use the office phones, but she felt Gloria should be an exception for today. Amazon was also Gloria's first Equity show. She had gotten a couple of "B" movies and some bit parts on television, but she was proud to have the legitimacy that she felt this stage play gave her. Though a bit high maintenance, Gloria was basically a kind person and had been trying to get Christine an interview with her agent. She saw Matthey and hung up the phone.

"Sorry, Matthey. I wanted to talk to Jeci. He heard my voice and just started sobbing. The service is Thursday at two o'clock. The First Sharon Baptist Church in Long Beach. I promised Jeci we'll all be there. We won't have rehearsal, will we?"

Baptist! Matthey wondered. "Of course not. We'll be there." She prayed Alan wouldn't start screaming about this one. "I know this isn't easy for you. Alan is very worried about you."

"He doesn't think I'm not doing a good job, does he?"

"No, no, of course not. He thinks you're fantastic. He just knows you're upset and wishes he could help you. He wants you to know that he understands how you're feeling and if you need any extra time before tonight's show, just let me know."

"Wow, Alan's such a sweetheart. I'll be alright. Thanks, Matthey. Oh, that sounds like Alan yelling for you." Her office, like the dressing rooms, had a speaker in the ceiling that broadcast the sound from the stage.

Matthey debated ignoring Alan and using the phone but her watch now indicated at least thirteen minutes of the ten-minute break had passed and she headed back out front. Tony caught her as she was trying to quickly pour herself a cup of coffee.

"Talked to Myrna. Last name is Reyes. Non-Equity. Myra told the guy managing her that if she didn't have a green card, no job. He swore it was no problem. So far there's no phone number or address. The guy calls her every hour. Says his phone is broken and he has to use different neighbours. Said they're in the process of moving. Must be her boyfriend too, huh?"

"Thanks, Tony. When we do the crowd scene tonight, make sure the guys know to fill in the spot where Christine was. We won't get Isabel until tomorrow. Go ahead and give the baby to someone else to hold just for tonight's preview. Oh, and if this manager--his name is Che--should call, try to get me or at least try to get a phone number and promise him I'll call right back."

"Sure. Sounds like Alan's having a stroke. Talk to you on headset."

Matthey ran to her seat in the back of the house. Alan was sputtering comments to the walls about starting rehearsal now that Ms. Cole had decided to honour them with her presence. Matthey got the stage into the right light cue and settled back in the darkened theatre.

What was Isabel like? She was going to have to be careful not to call her Jacqueline. Or maybe not. After all she'd never met her. She'd have to call Debbie and Ben soon. "Oh, God. I hope she's not using drugs."

"Matthey, you're mumbling again."

"Right."

Chapter Seven

It was 11:45pm when Matthey put her key in Bill's door. She
had knocked but only the dog scratching on the inside of the door
indicated that anyone had heard her. As she closed the door behind
her, she noticed the television was showing an old rerun of <u>Maverick</u>.
The show had been one of her favourites, when it was rerun the first
time.. Years ago. Must be cable. Lying sprawled on the floor
between the coffee table and the small couch was Bill. A glass of
vodka was next to him. The ice cubes had almost melted. As she
watched him, he began to snore. Deep, syncopated snorts that seemed
to begin in his toes. The dog was dancing around her willing her hand
to touch his body.

Matthey stood there for a minute deciding whether to stay.
Finally, the persistence of the sheltie persuaded her, and she put down

her purse and bag and dropped to her knees to give Brady his usual welcome.

"Hi, buddy. How you doing? Yeah, good boy." She rubbed his ears vigorously and hugged his whole body. "So, how long as he been out? I know. I guess I should be glad he tried to wait up for me. Come on, let's go out to the kitchen for a beer. Nope, nothing for you." Matthey opened the refrigerator door. "Oh, good, one Corona left."

Matthey took her beer and went into Bill's office, a small room adjoining both the living room and the only bedroom. She took out her phone and called home to check her machine for messages. There were three. From Che. He had called the theatre four times, but each time Matthey couldn't come to the phone and he claimed to be unable to leave a phone number. The first message on the answer machine included a phone number. Matthey called it immediately. After five rings, a Spanish speaking male voice answered and, in halting English, told her it was a wrong number. She gave him her name and Bill's number, anyway. She called back and hung up immediately when the same voice answered. Well, she thought, I guess I'll have to wait until tomorrow to meet Che.

She and Brady went back into the living room and sat on the small couch next to the, now silent, Bill. Brady hugged her side. Matthey stared down at Bill and tried to remember why she loved him. They had met two years ago when they were both on tour with Jesus Christ, Superstar. It was a five-week, eight city tour. Matthey was the production stage manager. The executive producer was also the producer of the Christian daytime soap, It's Your World. He had never been involved with legitimate theatre before but found out his soap's leading man could sing and decided to package the tour as a promotional gimmick to boost ratings. He insisted that they get a "pro" television associate producer to accompany the tour since TV was the only way he knew how to run a production. That person was Bill. He had an excellent reputation as a freelancer and was much sought after. Luckily his background had been in theatre and he knew the importance of a theatrical production stage manager rather than the TV stage managers the executive producer had intended to hire.

Bill had worked in New York with the master carpenter who was the union house man at the Emerson Theatre, also in downtown L.A. A year earlier Matthey had worked at the Emerson on a new musical about a Mormon who became a geek in a side show of a circus after being shunned by his church and turning to alcohol. It had been a difficult show to manage because of personalities which included the very wealthy CEO who was fronting all the money and knew nothing about theatre or producing. It was also made difficult because the script was an embarrassment to the paper it was typed on. It closed after two weeks to audiences of 40 in a house that sat 1500. Everyone but the producer was thrilled. Matthey had managed to keep her cast, director, and crew on an even keel and the master carpenter became a good friend. So, when Bill called asking for recommendations the first person he thought of was Matthey. She interviewed and got the job.

They flirted in Pittsburgh, started sleeping together in Chicago, declared their love for each other in New Orleans and talked marriage in Nashville. When they returned to Los Angeles, she moved in with him and they started house hunting. Two months later his father died. Alcohol had never been absent in their court-ship but now Bill started in on his bottle of vodka as soon as he came home from work and four nights out of the week Matthey would go off to bed alone leaving Bill passed out before the TV. She always covered him with a blanket. Sex became less frequent. Hell, it became almost non-existent.

Two months after that Bill's Aunt Lonya, his father's only relative, died. The same day Brady was hit by a car and developed an internal condition that meant Bill couldn't roughhouse with him anymore or take him for long walks. That night Matthey woke to the sight and sound of Bill sitting on his side of the bed pissing into the blanket that was laid on the floor for Brady to sleep on. Matthey thought it seemed awfully Freudian, somehow, and found it interesting that she wasn't disgusted. Bill remembered nothing in the morning and two weeks later she moved back into her Hollywood apartment.

A few months passed. He travelled on business a lot. And they started seeing each other again. This time she didn't move in. He agreed he should see a therapist but never had the time. He was more in demand as an associate producer than ever. He did find the time to see his internist whenever he felt the frequent aches, pains and fevers. He was convinced he would die before he was fifty. Sex was occasional. She knew she would leave him for good eventually but was trying to fall out of love with him first.

Matthey finished her beer and started shaking Bill. "Come on, Bill. Wake up. Let's go to bed."

Bill opened his eyes and attempted to comprehend where he was. "Comon. Schnuggle up her. Mishedya."

"No, Bill. Let's get up. Up you go. I missed you too." Bill tried to pull her down. "No, I'm not laying down. You're getting up. Let go, Bill!"

Matthey succeeded in getting him up to a sitting position with his back against the couch. As she steadied herself, ready to pull him up to his feet, she heard the phone ring.

"Letitring. 'chine's on. I'm too schrong foorya. Haha."

"I have to answer it. I've given your number to a few people at work." Matthey gently pulled away from his grip on her ankle. "Don't lay down!" She ran into the office to get the phone before the machine picked up.

"Hello. This is she. Che! Yes. You <u>did</u> get this number. Great! No. I don't have a script on me. Casting has one for you. Yes, I have my own script. Uh, Isabel will have plenty of time tomorrow to read the script and rehearse for her crowd scene. Hell, she doesn't even need a rehearsal for it. Yes, it's a good script. We're still doing rewrites, but a lot of people seem to like it. Yes, we've modified the nudity quite a bit. Che, it's after midnight. You really refuse to go in tomorrow and sign unless you've read the script first? If you give me an address, we can messenger one over to you first thing tomorrow morning. You'll be moving. Right. OK. Where are you all now?"

Matthey looked at her watch and yawned. "OK, meet me at <u>Charms</u> on Ventura Boulevard. It'll take you about twenty minutes to get there. Just west of Laurel Canyon on the south side. I'll be there in half an hour. If I'm late, wait. I'll get there. OK. See you both soon. Good-by."

Matthey went back over to Bill who was now snoring again, but still sitting upright. She shook him again. This time he seemed more amenable to her effort and he took her hand as she pulled him into the bedroom. She managed to get his socks and blue jeans off, leaving his underwear and tee shirt on. As she started to maneuver him under the covers Bill seemed to wake up a bit.

"Hi, darlin'," he mumbled a little less incoherently. "I tried to stay up. Where's Brady? Such a happy dog."

"I know darlin'. He's the best. I'm going to leave after I get you to sleep. I have to meet the manager of one of my actors. I have to show him a script. I'll probably just go on home after."

"No! I want you here. I'm sorry. I just got so tired."

"Bill, you drank too much. You always drink too much. I love you, baby. Just go to sleep now. I'll talk to you tomorrow."

"Come back here. Please. I need you." Bill had already closed his eyes.

"I'll talk to you tomorrow," Matthey whispered. She waited until his breathing slowed, then signaled for Brady to get on the bed. She turned off the light and closed the bedroom door on the two of them.

Standing in the bathroom brushing her teeth, she stared at herself in the mirror. A tired but attractive face, a face that looked younger than its years looked back at her. She sighed. She remembered a time when she would have stayed in that bedroom and Brady would run around in circles trying to find room to lay on the bed. Too much wriggling and squirming for him to settle in one place. Too many moans and giggles and wee hours discussions for any of them to get a decent night's sleep. Matthey rinsed out her mouth. That was a very long time ago. And for a very short period.

Matthey always figured that when they finally broke up some "good woman" would have him married and expecting their first child within a year. He would happily be going to his weekly AA meetings and they would run into her on the street and he would tell her "yup, ole Bess here made all the difference. Just swept into my life and cleaned me up. No nonsense about this woman. I tell you, Matthey, having a family makes all the difference. I hope you find out sometime. I really do."

Matthey splashed cold water on her face. "Fuck you," she said. Checked Brady's water dish and locked the front door behind her.

Chapter Eight

Matthey walked into the front door of <u>Charms</u> and quickly saw that Che hadn't arrived. Only three people were in the bar. An older man who looked either deep in thought or drunk and a couple in their fifties who were obviously enamoured with each other. <u>Charms</u> had a way of doing that. It had the best jukebox in town for forties music. She and Bill had often slow danced among the barstools. He could be a good dancer when sober.

Matthey walked up to the bar and ordered a double dry vermouth on the rocks with a twist. She paid and settled into one of the comfortable wooden booths that lined the wall opposite the long cherry wood and mirrored bar. She sat facing both the front and side doors. Matthey had often thought she must have been a gangster in a previous life. She could never comfortably sit in a room unless her back was against a wall and her body faced the majority of the room. This hadn't proved too inconvenient, but she had noticed in the last few years that longtime friends tended to adopt this same neuroses, and then claim that they had always been that way. She didn't care except that it led to subtle hostility when each felt they had a right to the secure position. Long time friends starting off a meal with one of them seething at being manipulated into being vulnerable to a mob hit didn't make for affectionate reminiscences.

Matthey was concerned that she give a professional impression to Che and Isabel. She didn't want to even suggest that her interest was about anything more than the play. She opened the script and decided to spend the time pretending to make notes.

"Matthey Cole?"

"Matthey looked up. "Yes.

"How do you do. I'm Che Gascon. I was in the restaurant section and saw you come in. I waited for you to get settled."

Damn.

"May I sit down?"

Damn. Damn. Damn. He was gorgeous! "Of course," Matthey said. He was drop dead, incredibly gorgeous! "Where's Isabel?" Black, thick curly hair. Eyes you could raise koi in.

"She's at home. We felt she should be rested for tomorrow."

A mouth you wanted to suck. "Sure, that's a good idea." Teeth you wanted to lick.

Che settled into the seat across from her. "I appreciate your meeting me at this hour. It's very gracious of you. I trust you weren't already in bed."

"No problem. This is on the way back home, anyway. Here's my script. It shouldn't take you too long to read it. It's a fairly short play."

"I'd hoped, perhaps, I could take it with me and return it to you at your convenience." He adjusted his leg and it now rested lightly against hers.

She held her breath for a beat. "No, that would be impossible. Everything is in that script. All the cues, charts. I never let my script out of my sight. Sorry."

"Well, if you don't mind waiting. I'm quite fluent in English but it does take me a bit longer to read it."

"You only have the slightest accent. Where are you from?" Oh, didn't you slip that in smoothly, Matthey thought.

"I was born in Madrid but I've traveled extensively. I learned my English when I lived in Edinburgh for two years."

"Yes, you do have just a hint of a Scottish accent. I never would have thought of it. How did you happen to end up in Hollywood managing actors?"

"Isabel is my only client. She's very talented. I'm very confident that she will be tremendously successful"

"I'm looking forward to meeting her tomorrow. I understand that she's from Mexico. What part?"

"Small town north of Puerto Vallarta."

Aha! Wouldn't happen to be Bucerias, Mr. Mysterioso? Matthey realized she was thinking in a John Wayne accent. "How long have you both been in the States?"

"Oh, I've been in and out for years. Isabel came up over a year ago."

"Really! I don't know why but I thought she was new into the country. I guess, because I heard she barely speaks English."

"She's working very diligently on her speech."

"You know the character only has a few lines, although she is on stage most of the play."

"Yes. I believe it will be a significant role for Isabel. Perhaps, I should read a bit of this." He shifted his foot away.

"Yes, of course. Can I get you something from the bar?"

"Thank you. Soda water would be very nice. Please get yourself another, as well. Tell the bartender to put them on my tab."

His tab? When did he get here? Matthey walked over to the bar and ordered the club soda. She brought it back to the table for Che, picked up her own drink and went back to the bar and hoisted herself up on one of the barstools. The couple looked at her briefly and went back to their mutual admiration. The elderly man never looked up.

"Excuse me," Matthey asked the bartender. "The gentleman in the booth, there, when did he arrive?"

"About fifteen minutes before you. He ordered and asked if he could look at a menu in the restaurant. I forgot he was in there.

"Thanks, just curious." Obviously, he didn't call from where he said he was. Matthey glanced over at Che who was intensely studying the script. She sighed. He was right. He didn't read very fast. Maybe he would skip the pages that didn't have Isabel's part in them. Somehow, she doubted it. Why didn't they just come to the performance earlier and watch the damn thing.

His profile was fantastic. Straight nose. Good chin. He didn't slouch. No squinting at the pages. She realized she was wondering what his ass looked like. Maybe he'd take his jacket off. She wondered if she was only imagining a bulge under his right armpit.

She hadn't talked with Debbie and Ben. She had managed to find one private minute during the dinner break when no one was in her office, but the landline had been busy. Debbie had never given her a cell number. She figured it would be more interesting talking to them after she had met Che and Isabel anyway.

"Excuse me, miss, but the gentleman is signaling to you." Matthey picked up her drink and went over to the booth.

"Surely, you're not finished already?"

"This scene. Between Jacques and Louis." Jacques was the plantation owner and Louis was his nephew. "Where they're discussing whether Danais should live in the main house." Danais was the young Brazilian girl.

"It seems a very contrived method of introducing the idea of conflict among the house-hands. Don't you agree?"

Jesus, it's just an understudy job. Your client should be grateful just to be offered the part without auditioning. But she admitted a slight feeling of smugness that he wanted her opinion.

"Yes, I definitely think so. I've mentioned it to the director. Actually, that's one of the areas that we should be getting more rewrites on for rehearsal tomorrow."

Che nodded, pleased, and Matthey went back to her barstool. Christ, he's really reading that thing. And he's not stupid. I wonder how he knows Isabel--Jacqueline? He's got to be in his early forties. Although if he said he was ten years either way I wouldn't be surprised. Isabel must be a knockout.

Fifteen minutes later he came over to her. This time Che brought the script. "Thank you. I believe I've read enough. It needs a considerable amount of work but that should be no problem. When is the opening?"

"A week from Thursday. We'll be doing rewrites up until then."

Che took his keys and money out of his left pocket. "That should be plenty of time." He put five dollars on the bar. "I wish to thank you again for being so generous with your time. I believe it will be a pleasure working with you and getting to know you much better."

The koi started frolicking with each other. "Definitely. I'm sure you and Isabel will find the Hopkins an interesting place to work. Rehearsal starts at one o'clock tomorrow and goes until six. Presumably, your contractual dealings will be ironed out and we'll see Isabel at one. Mostly she'll just be watching rehearsal and taking down blocking. The preview starts at eight tomorrow evening. Half hour is seven thirty. That means I expect her backstage, signed in by seven thirty. Although her actual crowd scene onstage is in the first act, I expect all understudies to stay in the theatre until their character makes their last entrance. In her case that's almost at the end of the play. During previews I expect understudies to stay until the end and be there for notes.

"Yes, I see." He stood, staring at her. "I believe you're good at your job, Ms. Cole. I like that. You're very beautiful. I'm surprised you're not an actress."

Matthey was satisfied to know she wasn't blushing. "I've always considered that comment an insult to the acting profession, Mr. Gascon. And to mine. But I suppose I should thank you".

"Yes. I'm parked in the valet lot. Would you like me to walk you to your car?"

"No, thanks. I'm right across the street."

"Good-by, then." Che turned toward the side entrance. "That was a delightful party, wasn't it?"

Matthey slipped her purse over her shoulder. "I beg your pardon?"

"Alex Golden's affair at his place in Malibu. You appeared to be enjoying the company of several people. I must say I was disappointed you never joined in a conversation with me." Che bent over to pick up a pencil that had slipped out of the script binder and fallen to the floor.

He had a great ass!

Che handed the pencil to Matthey. He ran his left thumb over her lips. "Fabulous mouth." And left.

Matthey ran across the street hoping to see which car the valet brought to him. But when she looked over, after what seemed a lifetime of pretending to prepare to start her car, he waved at her. There was still no car in sight and she couldn't possibly stay a moment longer. Damn. She drove back to her nice, quiet, dark house on Mt. Washington. Gaffer and Cristo were certainly happy to see her.

Chapter Nine

"I'm not here for the whole session. I'm just dropping off your tickets for Friday's preview. I'll pay you for this session but it will be my last. I wouldn't have come here at all but I forgot to cancel."

Dr. Tom was a different presence in his Beverly Hills office. His dark oak desk occupied three quarters of the space in the low-ceilinged room. On the couch, in front of the desk, Matthey felt like she was sitting in the back seat of a Volkswagen. Dr. Tom had told her she could always lay down and have all the leg room she wanted but she refused, for some good reason that she could never quite figure out. Today, he was dressed in blue jeans and an obviously new ski sweater. The temperature in the room seemed a bit warm, Matthey thought.

Dr. Tom smiled and leaned further back in his large matching oak swivel chair. "Matthey, I was hoping you weren't going to let our last little encounter overly influence your judgment on such an important matter as mental health. Especially yours."

"Dr. Tom, you must admit it was a little bizarre. You broke into my house, raided my freezer, erased my answer machine, slept in my bedroom and snuck out the next morning while I was there. You didn't even take your vomit-ridden clothes when you finally left. They're still in the driveway."

"Oh, I thought you might wash them. Oh, well, throw them away. Nothing can bother me today. I will concede that my visit to your temporary residence might be construed as being a shade out of the ordinary but I'm not an ordinary man. I'm not an ordinary psychologist. Yesterday, a woman came to me, suicidal. She had no family, no love, no self-esteem. All her goldfish had gone belly up, so to speak. This morning I sent her home a happily married woman with two kids and a thriving career in interior decorating."

"Husband and career, maybe. Far-fetched, but within someone's realm of reality. But two kids in twenty-four hours? Even God might choke on that one."

Dr. Tom poured himself a Perrier. "Oh, Matthey, Matthey, Matthey. You put up such a block to your own self-awareness. Well, that's your enjoining, of course. I should know. I speak from a mind-frame of Zen philosophy processed with Freudian theory. And, of course, smidgens of Jung, Thoreau, Plato and Jim Jones."

"Jim Jones! Are you out of your mind?"

"The Alaskan longshoreman. Nothing is written down, but if you travel throughout the Yukon, the people you talk to are always interspersing their conversation with pearls of wisdom culled from Jim Jones. He died when he took his dog sled into the Manicalbou

Glacier to hunt the presumably mythical Nobe, King of the Great Elk. He was never seen again."

Matthey tried sitting cross legged on the couch. She couldn't make it look natural. "You were talking about the suicidal woman."

"Yes. The husband, kids, career were all her dream, her goals. What she would have if her emotional growth hadn't been stifled, as a child, by her alcoholic mother. I was simply able to convince her, by doing a few basic exercises, that her mother, who is dead, has changed. Gone to the great AA in the sky, if you will. She is now an ideal mother and wants nothing more than for her baby girl to find the happiness and success that she really always wanted for her, if alcohol hadn't clouded her brain. I've shown my patient how to call on this ideal mother whenever she has need of love and comfort. She left here believing that she has a right to want to have a good husband and to be a mother. I'll need to see her for another, oh, twelve sessions, but by then she'll be secure in her pursuit of her goals.

"What if she never finds the husband and the kids?"

"Now, are we talking about her or are we talking about you?" Dr. Tom's ever-present smile grew deeper. But not deep enough to show the crooked tooth on the left side of his mouth, that he hated. He put his thumbs together and placed them under his fleshy chin, pushing up.

"That looks like a new sweater. A present?"

"As a matter of fact, yes, it is. I bought it for myself yesterday. As a reward. In a way, I have you to thank. What you describe as 'bizarre behaviour', I found to be a therapeutic release. I now realize I have depths inside myself I never knew existed. There's no telling the things I'm capable of. I spent five hours last night figuring out a formula for incorporating the need for such spontaneous acts into my psychological theories. I believe I can get a least three chapters out of it. I'm really so lucky. Most people spend years drifting, wondering how best to use what few talents they've been given. When I think of how many people my book is going to help. So many lost people, who otherwise would think muddling through life is the only choice. I think this is going to be my lucky sweater. I think I'll wear this sweater every time I sit down to write."

Matthey had shifted so she was sitting back on her heel, sideways, her right shoulder leaning against the back of the couch. She counted at least fifteen bears among his collection of stuffed animals. "Dr. Tom, you told me that someone called me while you were sleeping and mentioned something about play victory. Do you remember what time in the morning that was?"

"Well, I was asleep. I can't be sure of the exact time."

"I know. But was it three in the morning or eight in the morning? You must have some idea."

"Of course, I have an idea. I didn't fall asleep until around 2:30. I woke up around 7:30 and had something to eat. That's when I remembered having heard the phone ring and went in to check the machine. Instead of pushing rewind, I hit the erase button, by accident. So, I couldn't check it. Therefore, the call must have come after 2:30 and before 7:30. I then went back to sleep until your arrival."

"Hmmm. Probably after six. After I left. Che would have assumed I'd go straight home." Jason must have given him my number, she thought. Of course, I'm also listed in the phone book and my machine at the apartment has this number as a referral. "I thought you told me you intentionally erased my messages."

"I've become completely secure within myself, now. I no longer need to resort to fabrications to maintain my control. Who's

Che? Someone else you're sleeping with? I just bought a case of Trojans. I'll be happy to sell you a couple of boxes."

"No. Thanks. Tom, this is probably a mistake, but, in your opinion, using your theories, what kind of person ends up in life dealing drugs? I don't mean in a street corner sense, but someone who's intelligent, who could easily be successful in other fields."

"That would be a 'zap success' with, probably, a 'zap childish' mixed in. Someone who is afraid to be successful and therefore chooses a career that is invariably doomed to fall apart in his face. But someone who needs to be important and feels that having money and working hard will bring him comfort. He probably had a mother who encouraged him to stay with her. Who was unconsciously pleased when he wanted to quit piano lessons so he could spend more time with her. Grateful when he admitted he was scared to go away to Boy Scout camp. The father was, probably, a workaholic who only praised his son when he got A's. Frowned and told him he could do better when he brought home a B. So, this guy strives to be tops at something, which will please his father, but chooses a field that will ultimately ruin him, which he believes, somewhere buried in his psyche, will please his mother."

"Wow, that almost makes sense. Good. I'd hate to think I'd been a total fool to come to you." Matthey was now sitting hugging her knees.

"I wonder, if I buy six more identical sweaters, if they'll all be interchangeably lucky. And I can just wear this sweater forever. It can be my trademark. Noah Trevor will ask me about it. Women will send them to me."

"Thanks, Dr. Tom. I'll see myself out. Enjoy the show on Friday." Matthey scooted to the end of the couch and straightened her legs with relief. If she hurried, she could get to the theatre before ten.

Isabel should be coming in today and she hoped to get in a phone call to Debbie before she showed up. Before they showed up. At least that was one thing Matthey was sure of. Che was going to be around a lot. Hmmm.

Chapter Ten

"'decide…who…stays…up…and…who…stays, I mean goes…down' Yes, I'll hold." When Matthey arrived backstage at the theatre, Myrna phoned to tell her that Che and Isabel had just arrived in her office and were prepared to sign the contract. Did Matthey want to talk to them? She told Myrna, no. Just tell Isabel that she should be in the theatre at one o'clock for rehearsal.

Debbie came on the line.

"Matthey! It's great to hear from you so soon. I just wrote out your Christmas card last night. The kids are painting watercolors on the front of each one. I've picked out paintings from cities all over the world and we're matching each scene with each person."

"Sounds lovely. Maybe I'll think about Christmas when Thanksgiving is over. I try to wait and see if I get those free address stickers with my Christmas Seal solicitation before I get too serious over the endeavor."

"Oh, Matthey, you're too much. I know it seems a wee bit early, but this Syrian thing is making us all work such late hours. All I do is translate North Korean letters and telephone transmissions all day long. So far, I've been able to get my piano practice in, but I don't know how much longer I can keep that up. But, anyway, enough about me. Have you heard something?"

"Are you sure you don't mind this being taped? I could try to call you later at home?"

"Oh, I'm sure the government has their hands full with more important things than my little domestic intrigues. And, besides, I've found it's not too hard to make things disappear, if you know the right people. And the right person owes me a few favors. I'm making two dozen loaves of pumpkin bread for him to give to his nieces and nephews when he goes to Missoula, Montana for his grandparents seventy-fifth wedding anniversary. Can you imagine? Of course, the kids are upset that I'm using their jack-o-lanterns, but it's been three weeks since Halloween and I hate to waste things. We carved a pumpkin in the image of every president from Washington to Clinton. Hillary Clinton-I'm still confident. You should see the orange guy pumpkin. Hilarious. They were displayed on parents' night at the school and won first prize for most patriotic."

"I hope you took pictures before you cooked them."

"Oh, of course. Slides and we videotaped them. With accompanying music--all in the appropriate historical period."

"Right. Sounds great. Well, anyway. I've found Che Gascon and his friend, who might be Jacqueline."

Matthey heard a sharp intake of breath through the earpiece. How melodramatic, she thought. And how human, thank God.

"My gosh, really? I knew you could do it. You were always so clever. What's she like? Have you told her anything?"

"I haven't seen her yet. I expect her in at one for rehearsal. It turns out Che was at that party, at least I implied he was, and he either found out I was looking for him or else just decided to find out who I was, but I suspect he heard I was asking for him. Anyway, that's beside the point. Our understudy was killed in an automobile accident and Jacqueline, whom I assume is Isabel, had met our casting director earlier and she ended up getting the understudy part. I met Che last night to show him the script. He's very bright and incredibly good-looking. About forty, I think. He may be dealing coke, but I doubt that he's using it."

"And this Isabel is with Che and you think she's really Jacqueline?"

"What? Oh. Right. He's her manager. I haven't met her, but all the facts fit. The age, the town she comes from, she doesn't speak English well. However, she does have a green card, apparently, and Che told me she'd been here a year."

"Under Isabel's name?"

"I'm sure. Isabel Reyes."

"Well, I imagine I can check on that somewhere around here. See if immigration really issued one. Can you make a copy of the one she has?"

"Already asked casting to do that."

"You know, Matthey. Ben and I aren't really sure what we want to do about Jacqueline. The kids don't know anything and neither do either of our families. She has always been tucked away in a corner of our memory. A name to send a check to. Not even her name. A memory our bank balance could afford. We always assumed she would happily marry the boy next door and have babies and grow fat in Bucerias. Now, of course, Ben's worried his daughter might be in trouble, but I don't really know, to what extent, we want to involve ourselves in her life. I'm really trusting you to help us. If everything is on the up and up and she seems happy, then, maybe, it's better to let things go. But, if she's in a bad situation, then it's going to be pretty hard to ignore. I know Ben won't be able to do that."

"Don't worry, Debbie. I understand. I don't intend to tell anybody anything before talking with you. I probably won't be able to call you again today, at least not until it's really late back there."

"No, I don't want to wake the kids. Try to call me tomorrow. Oh, my code's going to change. It'll now be 'Tell...a...big...enough...lie...often...it...will...be...believed.'"

"Who makes up these things? A computer?"

"No. We all write them and put them in a shoebox and draw one out whenever someone decides we should change the code. At the end of the year, the one who's written the most used codes brings a cake in. Oh, that signal means they want to free up this line. I'll talk to you soon."

Matthey hung up and immediately dialed casting's number. "Myrna, hi. Were you able to make a copy of Isabel's green card? Great! Thanks. Bye." Myrna had copied the document when she had taken it upstairs to show to the general manager. The Hopkins had been burnt before. An actress in a leading role had sworn she had a green card and the afternoon of opening night it was discovered she had lied and the Actors' Equity Union had pulled her from the show. Management had no intention of letting it happen again. Matthey hoped they weren't.

"Excuse me. You are Matthey? I am Isabel Reyes."

Matthey looked up at the doorway to her office and saw a young girl that might have been taken for a senior at Beverly Hills

High School if it wasn't for the thick accent. She wasn't a knockout but she was fascinating. Very, very long but curly hair. Natural, not permed. Dark complexioned, but with cheerleader round, blue eyes. Matthey judged her to be about five feet two inches tall and less than one hundred pounds. But the weight was well distributed. No boyish waif, just a very budding young woman. Che may be robbing the cradle, but he could have done worse. Her manner seemed very tentative, but Matthey felt no instinctive urge to put her at ease.

Matthey didn't stand. "It's a pleasure to meet you. Have you signed your contract?"

Isabel nodded.

"I see Myrna gave you a script. The crowd scene that you're in comes about two thirds through the first act. We should be running through it this afternoon. As I told Che, you should be back here at one o'clock to watch rehearsal and take down blocking. Did he explain everything to you?"

"Yes. He will be with me to write. I am learning still."

"No problem. You'll learn most everything by watching, anyhow. But until opening night, the play will keep changing, so you need to stay on top of everything."

Matthey figured Isabel was getting the gist of what she was saying, judging from the intent, concentrated look on her face. And her responses.

"You'll be in dressing room number five. That's the large chorus dressing room which you'll share with two others. Here's an old contact sheet. I'll make up a new one with your name when I get a chance. You'll need to sign in on the bulletin board by the stage door each time you come in. No, not now, but when you report in for your rehearsal call. Just initial by your name. I also post the daily rehearsal schedule there. Here's an overall performance schedule. I'm going to need your address and phone number for the contact sheet."

"No lo comprendo." Matthey realized that Isabel never shifted her weight from one leg to the other. Not even slightly.

"It's alright. I'll get it from Che. Isabel, the woman you're understudying, Gloria, she was very close to Christine, the girl who was killed. The one you're replacing. It might take her a little while, but she's very sweet and I'm sure you'll eventually find her to be a good friend. We were all very fond of Christine and tomorrow's rehearsal will start later so that we can go to her memorial service. I won't expect you in until three o'clock."

"Yes."

"After rehearsal starts this afternoon, Tony, the assistant stage manager, will find you and get you together with the wardrobe mistress. I'm sure Christine's clothes will fit you but there'll probably have to be a few nips and tucks. In general, Tony is the one to ask any questions of during the rehearsal. I stay out in the house."

"The house?"

"The seats where the audience sits. We call that the house. It's only eleven thirty now so you're free to get some lunch. Nothing around here is terrific but it's all adequate."

"Che is taking me for lunch."

"Oh, great. Where are you meeting him?"

"Che is driving the car to box office, uh, curveover?"

"Turnaround. Just go back out the stage door and walk around the theatre to your left, that way, and you'll see it."

"Thank you."

"You're welcome. I'll see you in about an hour, then."

Isabel turned from the doorway and strolled out the back entrance. Matthey stood and watched her. If she was inclined to be unkind she might describe it as a saunter. It was her stance. There was nothing tentative about that. She stood like a woman who knows exactly where she's going. Like a woman who has eyes in the back of her head. A woman who knows the effect she has on people and who knows how to use it. Like most Beverly Hills high school seniors.

Che, Matthey thought, for shame. You even get the car for her. Bet, somehow, you've already got your hands on a Mercedes. Well, at least it will be fun watching your back while you take down Isabel's blocking. But, my dear man, I will have to draw the line at letting you hang out in her dressing room. Maybe, I'll let you use my office now and then, just to wait in.

Matthey figured she might as well grab a sandwich while she had a moment. Protein made her more alert. And she had a feeling she was going to have to be very alert for quite a while.

Chapter Eleven

"OK. That's it, everyone. Half hour is 7:30. Have a good dinner." Matthey snapped her script closed and started to race to the bathroom. It had been six hours and her bladder was screaming obscenities at her.

Annie grabbed her arm. "Did you get those last cue changes? I didn't have time to tell you about them earlier."

"No problem. All written in. Listen, I'm dying. I'll see you backstage." Matthey made it as far as the steps down to the lobby.

"Matthey. Do you have a moment?"

Matthey looked at Che heading up the steps. Her sigh wasn't entirely one of anguish. He had come to rehearsal dressed the part of the successful, hip 'man in the biz'. Casual silk shirt. Light mauve. Tight, very tight designer jeans. New Balance running shoes. Black. A calculated outfit that could easily reek of shallowness. It crossed Matthey's mind that a photo blowup would look great on her wall.

"Hi, Che. Yes. What can I do for you?" She tried not to bounce on her toes. Her bladder was not impressed with narrow hips.

"I apologize for Isabel being late. It was entirely my fault. It took forever for the valet to bring my car."

"Yes. I tried to explain to her that she needs to be responsible for herself in the future. If she ever thinks she's going to be late then she should call. That way I don't worry."

"Of course. I will see to it. I was wondering. I believe Isabel should have her own dressing room. It's very difficult for her to concentrate on the role when two others are in the same room chattering to each other. The one even had her phone playing music. I told Isabel I'm confident you can work something out."

"I'm sorry. There are no other dressing rooms."

"Dressing rooms number 2, 3 and 4 only have one person in them. Perhaps one of them can move in with the other and Isabel can occupy the single room. I need to spend so much time with her, also, helping her with her English. We'd dislike bothering anyone else with her lessons."

"No. Those women have their own rooms because they have significant parts in the play. Isabel is an understudy and all the understudies share a room. It's the same with the men. Besides, I think it will be good for Isabel to get to know the other cast members. I'm sure the other two ladies in her room will be happy to help her out. When we start understudy rehearsals, they're the ones she's going to be working with. Che, also, it's theatre policy that guests aren't allowed in the dressing rooms after half hour. And since she does share you shouldn't be up there unless the other women are asked and agree. You're welcome to use the green room at any time." Matthey's urine content was becoming more pressing than her image of the inside of Che's pants zipper.

"I see. Perhaps we can discuss this at another time. I can tell that you are rather preoccupied at the moment. I would very much enjoy having you join me for drinks after the performance this evening. I understand the director will give notes first. I've arranged for a friend to pick Isabel up. I believe you usually frequent a place called the 'Inside Passage'."

"Well, why don't you check with me after the performance. Sometimes, I end up staying here after actor notes and meeting with Alan and having tech notes. But, of course, it would be a pleasure to join you for drinks. Did Tony get an address and phone number from you?"

"Wonderful. We'll talk tonight. I look forward to it. And I'll make sure Isabel is back here promptly at 7:30. Please, I've kept you from your business too long. Adios."

Matthey watched him jump on the stage to greet Isabel, who was standing there waiting with her purse and coat. They walked off, his arm around her shoulder. Hers remained at her side. Matthey made it to the handicapped stall in the lobby bathroom with only seconds to spare.

Twenty minutes later she walked into the Hung Wo restaurant on Hill Street in Chinatown. Roger was already there, sitting in a booth at the rear of the restaurant. He'd left the side facing the entrance for her. Matthey looked at the back of his head and realized she probably knew this man better than anyone else in her life. He probably thought the same about her. So, she thought, as she walked to the table, does that mean anything?

"Hi, honeybuns." She kissed him on the top of his head. "I actually got here earlier than I expected. I went to the bathroom and when I came out everyone had disappeared. Great, eh?"

"Thanks for meeting me for dinner."

"No problem. Where's Denise?" Matthey ordered a Tsing Tao beer. Roger decided to have one, too.

"She's working late. And will probably stay over at her friend's tonight. I did it. I asked her for a divorce."

"Oh, my God. What did she say?" Where was that beer?

"She said she realized we hadn't been communicating too well, lately. And that maybe it wouldn't be a bad idea for us to live apart. She has a shot at assisting on a movie that will go on location during the hiatus. Mexico. Non-union. I'm sure she'll get it. The production manager calls her all the time. I think he has the hots for her."

"Maybe she's good at her job. Was she upset? Are you guys really talking divorce or just trial separation?"

"I just said, I asked her for a divorce. When she left this morning, she took a suitcase with her. She said she hadn't thought about divorce but she sure didn't seem all that distraught at the idea."

"Of course, she's upset. But you've been thinking about this for months and she's got to have picked up on your feelings. Maybe she's just accepting what she knew was a foregone conclusion, anyway. If you guys can end this and remain friendly it'll be better all around."

"I don't know. You and I were friendly when we broke up. Maybe divorce should be ugly and bitter and filled with accusations. Maybe that validates the marriage, somehow. I don't want to be someone who just has friendly relationships with women. Maybe, I'm incapable of loving anyone. Of feeling deeply about anyone."

"Now, come on. We had lots of vicious fights. Remember, in Pennsylvania, when you tried to jump out of the car on the freeway?" Matthey spied the water. Thank God, there's the beer.

"No, you were the one who would yell and scream and act despicably. I'd just try to avoid any confrontation."

"Thanks. I can't say I remember it quite that way but I'm glad you think I did something right in our marriage. Do you want to order? Mu Shu chicken and spicy eggplant?"

"Oh, sure." Roger sighed and stared at her for a moment. "I know you think I've been joking about this for months. but it does look like I'm about to be single again. I want you to move in with me. We'll get a bigger house. You can pick it out. With your down payment and what I get from selling mine we should be able to afford a three bedroom. And you should really start trying to get pregnant as soon as possible. You told me your mother had a hysterectomy when she was forty. And my sister-in-law says she's getting hot flashes."

"Your sister-in-law is only thirty-seven. That's impossible."

"Her doctor agrees with her. My brother's just glad they had the baby last year. Originally, they had only wanted two, but now he's happy to have a third running around."

"And if she hadn't entered menopause, he would have been contented with just two?"

Matthey picked up her chopsticks and started rubbing them against each other to smooth out any splinters.

"This is depressing. I am not menopausal, and my gynecologist says I'm perfectly healthy. Roger, I want a baby, but I don't want to have one out of desperation. Matthey signaled the waiter for another beer. She started chewing on one of the chopsticks.

"I don't know. You might be right. Maybe we would be good together. I suppose we have matured somewhat. But shouldn't we get back together because of some kind of joyous desire on our part rather than just some acceptance of a sort of inevitability. Or maybe I'm being naive. Still believing in knights in shining armor. I mean...I know that the original feeling of falling in love, that desire to spend every waking second touching each other, I know it fades away. I know it never lasts beyond a few months. But they always talk of that feeling settling into some deeper, more meaningful kind of love."

Matthey thanked the waiter for the beer as he sat it down on the table. "Of course, all those 'they' people who talk like that have all been married for twenty years and have had two affairs or never have orgasms or bicker constantly so, maybe, that deeper love is really a myth and just a rationale for a fear of being alone. And if we admit, up front, we're afraid to grow old alone then, maybe, our relationship would actually be a more open and honest one. I haven't a clue what I'm really talking about."

The waiter placed the two dishes on the table. Both Matthey and Roger remained silent while he prepared the Mu Shu. He placed one on each plate. They both thanked him when he finished. Matthey immediately began stuffing her face. Roger watched her.

"I think we should go through therapy. You're the only one I've ever really enjoyed spending time with. You're the only one who can make me feel better about myself. Why don't we go back to the theatre, pull out the couch in the office and have a quickie? I haven't seen those cheeks in a long time."

"We did that once, four year ago, and the security guard walked in on us. And the couch can't pull out now. The desk blocks it. And I can also make you feel horrible about yourself. Remember San Francisco? Listen, Roger, I meant what I said Monday. Don't pressure me. I realize I can't wait forever to make up my mind about my life but right now I need to think about a few things. I want some time. Guilt-free time. OK? I know this is a difficult period for you, but I'm afraid you could sway me to make a decision that would be based on my feeling sorry for you instead of what's right for me and us. So, promise, no pressures!"

"I won't. But, if you reach any decisions, you'll promise to say something and not tell me, 'well, you never mentioned it again, so I thought you must have changed your mind?'"

"I wouldn't do that."

"Yes, you would."

"OK, I would. But I won't. Now, do you think we can actually eat and stop talking. We've got fifteen minutes. You're going to finish your beer?" Matthey cracked open one of the fortune cookies that were placed there.

"What's it say?"

"You will soon meet a dark stranger. Listen wisely and talk softly."

Roger leaned back and grinned. "Couldn't have said it better, but, hey, no pressure here."

Matthey fixed herself another Mu Shu Chicken. The problem was there were too many dark strangers. Including herself. She hoped she was listening wisely.

Chapter Twelve

By the time Matthey reached her seat in the booth, Tony was already on headset announcing that the actors were in place for the second act. She grabbed her handset as she flipped the cue light switches to the on position.

"Hi, just got here. I ran across the catwalk. Dropped a pencil, hopefully into someone's lap and not their eye. Stay on headset, OK, until I get the show started."

Matthey glanced at the clock and jotted down the time. After also writing down the length of the intermission she cleared her stopwatch. "OK. Warning on House to 1/2, House out, Lights 73, Sound J, Lights 73.5 and 74, Sound K, K down, L, Lights 74, Video 3 and 4, Lights 75, 75.5 and 76, Sound M through M4 and Video 5. Warning follow-spot, frame 3, in a head, on Victor, up left. Warning--"

"Who's Victor? What followspot?" The sound operator's voice spat out from the biscuit attached to her handset. Although headsets were the usual equipment in theatres, the Hopkins offered the opportunity of using a handset instead. She loved the freedom of being able to hear the show out of both ears and not be continually attached to a cord.

"Oh, sorry, Ronny," Matthey replied. "Must be thinking of another show. Sure glad you're around to catch these things."

"Nobody likes a smartass, Cole."

"Just wanted to see if you guys were listening to me. Sitting up here in this booth can get lonely. Wish we could all be in one room. I never see you guys. You're just disembodied voices. For all I know you could all be sitting in the crew room watching television with your headsets on. I say "go" and you just push a button and return to watching reruns of 'Seinfeld'. I could scream up here and no one would hear."

"Wear your headset like a normal person and I promise I'd check on you at the first commercial," said the voice of Charlie, the electrician. He was seated at his light board located ten feet up in the stage right wing.

"Would anyone like to start the second act? Save the philosophy for the drinks at the Inside Passage which presumably we'll have time for if we ever start this show?" Matthey forgot that the lighting designer kept a headset next to her during previews.

"Sure, Annie. Put art before life."

"Excuse me, Matthey. I just wanted you to know that we are all present in the stage right wing. Thank you."

"Carole, what are you doing on headset? Nevermind, OK, warnings on everything. House to half, Go."

Matthey looked out her tiny two feet by twp-foot square window at the audience below. "Yeah, guys. Run to your seats. Oh, think you can keep talking, Mr. Orange Dude. House out, Lights 73, Sound J--Go. Hah! Now try to find your seats in the dark. Dum-da-dum-da-dum-da-dum. Lights 73.5--Go. Lights 74 and Sound K--Go." Matthey finished the rest of the sequence of cues, adjusted the timings of the intermission on her performance report and asked if Tony was still on headset.

"Right here. You certainly sound like you're in great humor. Problems?"

"No, not really. I just gave this big spiel to Che this afternoon about not going up to Isabel's dressing room and Gloria caught me as I was heading up to the booth just now and tells me that when she came up for her costume change she found Che and Isabel in her dressing room sitting on the couch. They said they wanted a quiet place to run lines, but Gloria thinks she interrupted something. Said they looked too startled. Apparently, they said they didn't realize she would come back to her room once the show started. Oh, shit, Lights 76--Go. Warning on Lights 77 and Sound N. So, anyway, would you check and make sure Isabel is watching the show from the house like she's supposed to be and check that Che isn't anywhere near any of the dressing rooms?"

"Who's this Che guy?" Charlie asked.

"Oh, he's the new understudy's manager. They're both new to theatre and don't understand the protocol. He's basically OK."

"Is that the guy walking around backstage in designer jeans, acting like he owns the place?" the prop man whispered from backstage. That meant Carole was no longer on headset. Good.

"Yeah, but really, he's OK. He just needs to understand some rules."

"I'll teach the asshole some rules."

"No, Jay. I'll handle it, thanks. Tony, just keep an eye out. And have a shot of Bushmills waiting for me after the show."

"I'll watch carefully for Mr. Gascon, also."

"Carole! What headset are you on? Never mind. Uh, thanks, but just tell Tony if you notice anything." Matthey called the next two cues.

She hung up her handset and leaned back. If she scrunched down a little, she couldn't see the stage at all. Just the top half of the Brazilian jungle cyc. And if she squinted and tuned out the actors' voices, she could almost pretend she was all alone swinging from tree to tree with the two-dimensional monkeys that the scenic artist had painted on the backdrop. Annie's back lighting and the ever-present sound loop of jungle ambience caused her sweat glands to shift up a gear.

"Kreep, kkkreep. No, that's not how monkeys sound. Brawk, urawwk. No! They don't squeal. What the hell do monkeys do? Come on. Everyone does monkeys. It's like cows and sheep. Oh, Matthey, your memory's going fast. Must be age. Probably Alzheimer's. Or brain tumor."

The biscuit barked at her. "Do you want me to go on sound?"

"Matthey grabbed the handset. "Christ! Yes! Go! And, uh, warning Lights 78 and Video 6. Lights 78 Video 6--Go!. Thanks, Ronny." Matthey put the hand set back and found her place in the script. Pay attention, kid, she said to herself, this still pays the rent."

Matthey suddenly became aware someone was standing behind her. She whirled her stool around and knocked over her coffee cup that was sitting on the table by her right shoulder.

"Excuse me. I didn't mean to startle you."

"Che! What the hell are you doing up here?"

"I wanted to tell you that I must cancel the invitation that I extended to you that you join me for drinks tonight. I must attend to some personal business. I received a phone call and must leave immediately. I didn't want to depart without talking with you personally."

Matthey took a deep breath. "You should never walk across the catwalk during the show. The audience can hear you!"

"I can assure you, no one heard anything." He refrained from pointing out the obvious to her. "This is rather a grim, little place you have up here. It appears rather remote."

Matthey felt silly. "You know, you should not be up here. Completely against the rules. We have no insurance if you get hurt so I'm making it clear you've been given no authourity to be here.

He pointed to her script. "Don't you have a cue coming up?"

"Yes, I was just going to warn it." Matthey shifted slightly, her peripheral vision watching both the stage and Che. She felt sillier. She stayed in that position through light cues 81 and sound cues P and Q.

"Look, Che," Matthey said, swinging back around. "You shouldn't be up here, just like you shouldn't be in Gloria's dressing room. Isabel should still be watching the show at this point. She only has about forty lines, but she still has to watch the blocking. The role is onstage almost all the show. She also needs to get a sense of the overall direction of the show."

"She's sitting in Row P. And, of course, you're right. Can you actually see the stage from that small window? Do you mind if I look?"

Somewhere in her mind, Matthey started to protest as Che edged up to her left and hunched over. His face was inches from hers. She could smell his aftershave. English Leather. How common, how passé. How did he know it was the only scent that had faithfully driven her out of her mind since she was thirteen and had gone away to camp and developed a huge crush on one of her counselors who drenched himself in the stuff. Shit.

"Oh, look, there's Isabel sitting over there." He pointed, waiting for her to acknowledge the truth of his statement. Matthey nodded, trying to breathe without inhaling. His right arm reached easily around and rested on her right shoulder. Casually.

"Is that the keystep or only a jammer," Che asked? Matthey felt his breath on her hair. Without thinking she turned to him to say

"What?..what on earth are you talking about?" Only she never said it. Che's mouth was waiting, and it seemed the most natural thing in the world to let it meet hers. Oh God, his mouth was warm and soft and insistent. And he smelled so good, and he was so close, and the room was dark. She allowed her tongue to explore every corner of his mouth, only stopping when his demanded equal time.

"Matthey, hey, Matthey, you got a second?"

Matthey spun around. "Oh, my God!" She grabbed the handset. "Did I miss a cue? Which one? Tony, what is it?"

"Hey, calm down. Everything's fine. What's the matter? You fall asleep?"

"Oh, God!"

"I just wanted to let you know that there's a cop down in our office waiting to talk to you. It's about Christine's accident. He says he just wants to ask you a few questions. I didn't want you to be surprised by this guy who, by the way, could be right out of central casting. Detective O'Mally. Honest to God. You're going to love him."

"Thanks, Tony. I'll be there as soon as the show comes down. Take care of things with Alan, OK?"

"Sure thing."

Matthey put down her handset and turned around. Che was gone. She stood up to check if he was hiding in any of the corners of the room. He wasn't. She sat back down and, once again, found her place in the script. She reached for her coffee and remembered it had spilled. No matter. The rug was the owner of many stains.

She stared at the stage. Stared at Isabel. And felt her swollen mouth.

Chapter Thirteen

Matthey turned into her office and almost tripped over the feet of a tall, rather obese man who had a yellow and orange checkered sports jacket carefully draped over his knees. He was sitting on the chair just to the left of the door. It wasn't a comfortable chair and the couch next to him was empty.

"Officer O'Mally? Hi. I'm Matthey Cole. I understand you want to talk to me?"

"Detective Mally. Not O'Mally. Just Mally. Derivative of Malkovich. My grandfather changed it when he came over."

"Sorry. Officer Mally." Matthey put her script down on the desk. "What can I do for you?"

"Detective Mally. Do you mind if I shut the door?"

"Oh, sure. Uh, you'll have to get up. I have to move that chair to close the door. Sorry."

There were approximately five square feet of free space between the couch, chair and desk. Matthey felt like Mohammed Ali on roller skates as she attempted to maneuver around his bulk while he managed to consistently stand in the wrong place. She wished he'd sit on the couch.

"Please, feel free to sit on the couch." He didn't. She finally managed to find room for both Mally and the chair and still clear the pathway of the door. She closed it on Tony as he started to enter. He raised his eyebrows, questioningly, and then signaled his amusement at the situation. Matthey then danced around Mally again until he settled himself back in the chair after pulling it back to its original position. She started to sit down at the desk but spotted the poured glass of Bushmills on the phone table next to the couch. She settled herself next to it.

"It's been a long day. Do you mind?" She indicated the liquor as she swallowed it. Detective Mally took out a notebook from his jacket pocket. Matthey put the glass back down.

"I understand you have some questions about Christine's accident," she said. "Have you found the guy that did it?"

"Miss Cole, we have reason to believe that the person who hit Christine Ruis was deliberately trying to kill her. Do you know any reason why someone might want to do that?"

Matthey stared at him for several seconds. "No! No, no one would want to do that. The driver was just probably drunk? Everyone liked Christine. She was sweet, nice, friendly. We liked her boyfriend. She'd bring in pastries from her aunt's bakery shop. She'd make the coffee in rehearsal when the pot was empty. They were good, too...the pastries, I mean." Matthey was aware she was rambling. Let's see, when was Christine killed? Sunday night, what was I doing then? This is ridiculous. I don't need an alibi. Wait, I was at the party. Jason can vouch for me. Hey, so can Che, for that matter. "Why do you think it was deliberate?"

"We found the hit and run car. Abandoned. Just off the next freeway exit. It had been reported stolen an hour before the accident."

"Some kids, joyriding, and got scared?"

"It was stolen from the garage under the Hopkins Theatre. The owner was here at the play. Discovered it right after the show. He phoned the police immediately. He remembered parking next to a yellow Honda Civic."

Christine drove a yellow Honda Civic. Matthey started to get excited. "So, you find it a little coincidental that someone would steal

80

a car from a theatre parking lot and then happen to use it to kill someone who worked at the same theatre. This means the guy waited around in the stolen car until Christine got through with notes. Seems like a big risk. He'd have to assume the car would be reported as stolen. Of course, one could also assume it would take awhile before a general report went out over the police network. Except I remember one time several years ago when I was doing this show--"

"When was that?"

"When was what?'

"When did this show end?"

"Well, the show came down, then, around ten o'clock. Notes lasted around forty minutes, so...eleven o'clockish, I guess."

"Is there anyone who would profit from her death?"

Matthey drank some more Bushmills. "You mean, here at the theatre? No! She was the understudy. Absolutely no guarantee that she would ever go on. She probably wouldn't have. Our runs aren't that long."

"Who's the girl she was understudying?"

"Oh, no. Gloria and Christine were good friends. She was even trying to get her agent interested in Christine. There was no threat from Christine. Christine knew she was not very experienced and welcomed any advice she could get."

Mally spent several minutes scribbling in his notebook. He used a very stubby Black-wing pencil. The kind Norman always insisted upon using. Matthey moved the battery-operated pencil sharpener over to the shelf next to him. He grunted his acknowledgment and didn't use it. Still writing, he asked, "Anyone involved with the production dislike her for any reason? Jealous of her for being too likeable? Interested in her in more than a friendly way? Not like her background? Anything? Maybe someone in the box office or an usher that she offended or the woman who cleans her dressing room?"

"A man cleans the dressing rooms."

Mally stared over at her with no evidence of an expression.

Matthey shrugged. "Sometimes his wife helps. I'm sorry, I can't think of anyone. Everyone liked her. She was 'Little House on the Prairie' moves to Alhambra. Her boyfriend adored her. We adored them adoring each other. She liked animals. We used to talk about which commercials made us cry the most. Purina's or the telephone company's."

Tony knocked on the door. It was a bit too loud and too slow. Matthey wondered what he thought they were doing in there.

"Yes," Matthey called out. "What do you need?"

"Uh, Alan wants to know if we'll be able to repaint the fence post before the show tomorrow night. He says he's realized it's too white and that's what making the apology scene seem too insincere. He wants it more beige."

"Tell him, no problem. There's a paint call tomorrow. I'll tell Ralph. Notes still going on?"

"Yeah, probably another ten minutes. Nothing too important. Should be only a few rewrites for tomorrow. He wants to re-block the curtain call. Uh, are you going to be done soon? I'm supposed to call someone before 10:30 and tell him when to meet me.

Matthey looked over at Detective Mally. He frowned and scribbled in a comment next to the two lines he had written while Tony talked. Then he cleared his throat and closed the notebook.

"Yeah, Tony. We should be through in just a minute. OK?"

"Fine. I can go out to the fountain to call. Need anything?"

"No, thanks. I'll be out in a bit." She heard Tony walk back down the hall toward the stage. Mally was now standing and quite effectively blocking any pathway from the couch to the door. If she stood her face would be inches from his. She decided he must be aware of this and intentionally intimidating her. Matthey chose to look properly intimidated.

"I'd appreciate it if you kept your eyes open for any signs of anything unusual. I'd also appreciate your letting me know immediately if you think of anything or hear anything that might even remotely be of interest to me." He handed her a card. It just had his name and a phone number on it.

"I'd also like to ask you to keep our conversation between us. If there is anyone with the production that's involved, I'd rather they not be aware of any suspicions."

"Fine. I won't say a word. But I'd try another direction, if I were you." Matthey stood up suddenly, hoping to startle him into moving. He didn't. She lifted up his arm and ducked under it. He turned around to face her.

"Remember, if you have any thoughts, tell me. Don't take a chance of getting yourself into trouble."

Matthey turned her back to him while she put his card in her purse. She glanced up in the mirror and noticed him watching himself in the mirror. She saw him suck in his gut. She also noticed the bulge under his shirt when it tightened momentarily. Well, no mistaking that, Matthey thought. Guess Che didn't have a gun.

"Don't worry, Detective Mally. If I get into trouble, you'll be the first person I'll call." She opened the door and stepped out into the hall. He followed her out, an awkward move necessitating moving his chair away from the wall again that he did very quickly. She thought she saw someone duck around the far corner. Probably Tony. She noticed Mally look around, also.

"Remember, anything at all, call." There was no hint of a suggestion in his voice. It was all command.

"Of course. And please keep me posted if you have any new developments. I'd only known Christine for a few weeks, but I was fond of her and I'd really hate to think her death was anything but an accident."

Mally made one last notation in his notebook and put it away in his shirt pocket. He took his time putting on his jacket. Matthey watched him leave and then went back into the office and sat at her desk. Tony appeared seconds later. "Is he gone? What did he want? Could you believe that outfit?"

"He actually moves rather well in it, though, don't you think? Uh, apparently, the car that hit Christine was stolen. So, he had to ask some routine questions for the report. Go ahead and use the phone. I'll go handle the notes."

"They're finishing up," Tony said over his shoulder as he dialed.

Matthey headed down the hall toward the stage. She hated not being honest with Tony. She believed in telling her assistant everything, but this was out of the realm of any normal production problems. She'd always trusted her instincts. And her instincts told her to mull all this over for awhile. And not talk to anyone.

Chapter Fourteen

An hour later Matthey pulled into her driveway. She went around to the back of the car and pulled a bag of cat litter from the trunk. Automatically, she looked up at the windows on the house next door. Usually, Mr. Chan, the owner, heard her car and came to the windows to check on her. They had only exchanged a couple of words, but he seemed to feel it was his neighbourly duty to watch over her. This evening he was nowhere to be seen. Matthey closed the rear trunk and headed for the front door. Unlocking it, she was surprised to see both cats sitting on the chair across the room. Normally, Gaffer and Cristo would greet her at the door, dancing around, meowing for food.

She put her purse and bag of litter on the couch and went over to the cats. "Hi, guys. What's the matter? Not hungry, huh? Don't want any food?"

At the familiar word both cats jumped up. "Alright, that's better, guys." Matthey went into the kitchen and opened up the refrigerator to get the can of cat food. A six pack of Mabel's Black Label stared back at her. Matthey knew she had never bought Mabel's Black Label in her life. She didn't even think they made it anymore. An awareness of fear began enveloping her body.

At the same moment she realized she was smelling a residue of cigarette smoke. Then she heard a snort, a harumph and a whinny came from her bedroom. The only way to leave the kitchen was to pass the open bedroom door. She knew, without a doubt, that a hollow-eyed, gaunt, psychopathic serial killer would leap at her the instant she tried to run. She didn't move.

When Matthey was four and living in a small town in Ontario, Canada she was walking home one day after visiting her best friend, three and a half year-old Little Brayton. (His uncle was Big Brayton.) She came to an intersection one block from her house. A large truck was parked on the other side of the road facing the opposite direction of Matthey. Not just a big truck but a huge, monstrous king of the highways hundred-wheeler with mud and ice thrusting from its underbody. Deep in the soul of her gut, she knew that iron icon would make a pancake of her body as soon as she started across the street. It wasn't conjecture to the pre-schooler, it was pure, simple truth.

For thirty minutes she stood on the curb, her heart pounding, her mind racing around her head like a trapped hummingbird. There was no thought of escape. Of crossing the other way and heading home on the other side of the street. Or heading back and going around the block the other way. Matthey realized this was a test and she had to face it.

Finally, stoically summoning all her courage, she stepped off the sidewalk onto the street. That very instant the engine of the truck started. The four-year-old broke into a hysterical run and fell flat on her face in the middle of the road. Dragging herself on her hands and knees she reached the other side as the truck slowly shifted into gear. Once home, she snuck up to her room and changed clothes so her mother wouldn't question her about the cuts and bruises.

Matthey knew she had narrowly escaped death by listening to her instincts then, and she was listening to them now. She also listened to the absence of her breathing as she stood frozen by the refrigerator. She picked up a frying pan when she realized Gaffer had just slipped into the darkness of the bedroom.

"Matthey, you home? Justa sec, I'll be right out." Matthey slammed down the frying pan, causing Cristo to jump up to the counter.

86

"Fitzpatrick, is that you? What the hell are you doing here?"

Timothy Fitzpatrick stumbled into the light of the kitchen, rubbing his eyes with one hand and scratching his crotch with the other. On the bottom he wore maroon pajamas. On top was a Cub's tee-shirt. As usual, it was a size small. Fitzpatrick felt that skintight tee-shirts cleverly disguised his more than adequate girth. He also thought a little bloated skin showing between shirt and pants was sexy. No one had bothered spending any time attempting to dissuade him.

Matthey waited while he grabbed a paper towel and heartily blew his nose. She poured herself some Bushmills. Timothy had quit drinking hard liquor five years ago, after his wife left him and took their five kids to Alaska. Six months later he finally got a play professionally produced. It was well received. It was the twenty-third play he had written. The title was if be I, it ain't you, and was a rock musical about G. Gordon Liddy going back in time to 10,894 B.C. and leading the Ugga tribe to victory over the more advanced but also more hostile Kusskuss clan. The critics took it as a political satire. Matthey had stage managed it as a favour to the producer whom she had dated once.

"Matthey, you look great, great! It's so good to see you. What can I say? This is fabulous. Fabulous!" Fitzpatrick talked like a cuckoo clock on speed. "Well, you see, it's just crazy, crazy! I was in rehearsal and the lead decided that three months in Mt. Angel, Oregon would ruin his marriage and he left two days ago. And yesterday, the female lead said she saw the ghost of a nun hanging from her bedroom light and she left. We called a few people down here but no one would come up, so they cancelled my play and I started driving south at three o'clock yesterday morning. It was a tragedy, tragedy!

But it's O.K. I have a new idea. These things happen for a reason, yes. Yes! So, I'm back!"

Matthey finished her drink. "Uh, I'm sorry about your play, but, uh, you said you'd be gone for three months and it's only been two weeks."

"Matthey, I know. And I've figured it out. You can still stay here. We can share the bed. I won't touch you, I promise. We'll draw a line down the middle of the bed. O.K., or, or--you can sleep in the bed and I'll take the couch, or I'll take the bed and you can have the couch. Whatever you want. I said you could have this place for three months and you can. You can have it more! Matthey, your vibrations are still good. Your vibrations have always been good. Great!"

Matthey sighed and slumped against the sink. "Uh, Fitzpatrick, I appreciate it, but your couch is a park bench with foam rubber and throw pillows. You know, not quite so restful. Sharing a bed is not, uh, a good idea. And I really can't see crashing on that box spring in the back room. Unfortunately, I have someone staying in my apartment for two more weeks so I'm kind of in a bind. However, I'm sure I can work things out. I'll need to leave my stuff here for awhile. But I'll take the cats and leave tonight."

Fitzpatrick looked genuinely alarmed. "No, no, no! I'll leave! I'll go!" He began rocking.

"Wait, hold on, stop!" Matthey jumped forward and touched his jiggling stomach. Fitzpatrick froze. In the last year he had developed a theory that women were charged with an electrical impulse that was capable of killing brain cells. He believed this charge entered him when a female touched him. He was terrified of losing any more brain matter than the billions of cells he'd already drunk away with Jack Daniels. Matthey waited until the playwright relaxed and started breathing again.

"I don't think she got any. Amazing! Amazing!" he muttered holding the top of his head.

"It's alright, Timothy. Don't worry. I'm not upset. O.K.? Really. I'll go stay at Bill's. It'll be fine. Just let me get a few things. I'll come back on Monday to get the rest of my stuff and we can have lunch, alright?"

"You're sure this is right? You're the greatest, greatest! I'll buy you lunch. Yes. I'll do that. This is great. We'll have lunch. I'll tell you about my idea. It's wonderful, fabulous." Fitzpatrick concluded with an enormous yawn.

"Listen, you've been driving for hours. Go back to sleep. I'll call you tomorrow."

The forty-five-year old Irishman nodded and yawned again and wandered back into the bedroom. As he lay down, Matthey heard him mumbling "great vibrations, always did."

It took her twenty minutes to pack a couple of suitcases and put them and the cats in the car. She drove off, heading for the valley. The moon was waning. The classic rock station was playing all of Derek and the Dominos. It was a beautiful night for driving in Los Angeles.

Chapter Fifteen

At least for about ten minutes. As Matthey approached the entrance to the Glendale Freeway, she began to become aware of the possibility that someone was following her. Shit! Just as the radio had started playing "Layla". Double shit!

An involuntary shiver went through her. Glancing over at the cage that held the two cats she noted with satisfaction that the front of the carrier was securely butted against the dashboard. No great potential of the cats being too badly shaken up. She thought about buckling up herself but decided not to. Matthey had always hated that feeling of being confined. But she did lock her door.

It was impossible to tell what kind of car was behind her. It looked like a dark colour and had only one working headlight. Even during her hitchhiking days in college, she never got in a car with only one headlight. Just never felt right. Probably missed a lot of good rides, she thought.

Matthey signaled the left for the freeway entrance. The car followed her into the turn left lane, staying two car lengths behind. There was no other traffic. None on the freeway.

They idled, together, at the light. When the arrow and green light blinked on, she moved, suddenly, to her right, going through the intersection. The one-eyed shadow followed. No doubt now. Gaffer stood up with the abrupt movement and registered her disapproval. "I know, kid, I'm not thrilled, either. Just keep your brother from getting sick, O.K.?" Matthey looked for a gas station. An open one. San Fernando Blvd. was a major street but a rather deserted one this time of night. On her left was the Los Angeles River. On her right, small residential streets of Glendale. She was fairly sure she'd eventually run into a service station or all-night diner.

"Maybe it's Dr. Tom trying to earn another sweater. No, he'd never be caught dead in a car like that. And this guy is cool. He knows I know he's following me and he, apparently, doesn't care."

At that moment, Matthey felt her head brush the bottom of the sun visor as the cyclops behind rammed into her. Both cats stood up and protested. Again, her body whipped forward as he did more damage to her rear. The cats crouched down, quiet. Matthey jammed her foot on the accelerator and leapt ahead, cursing herself for not having her seatbelt on. She whipped a right on Central taking her below Forest Lawn Cemetery, heading north.

Quickly, she made a left at the end of the first block and, just as quickly, made a right at the next. She had no idea where she was going. Hopefully, she could evade him and, hopefully, she wasn't going to end up on a dead-end street. She knew he'd caught the first two turns. Matthey made three more fast turns, and not seeing any headlight behind her pulled in front of a station wagon parked halfway down the block in front of a small Spanish style home. She turned off her lights and waited.

Within seconds a car pulled into the intersection behind her. It idled there, presumably allowing the driver to look down both sides of the street. It backed up a few feet, as if to get a better view. The driver was on the side farthest from her, but she could tell the car was a four-door sedan, probably American, and seemed to be green in the moonlight.

Matthey took the moment to fasten her seatbelt and check the cats. When she looked back the car was gone. She decided to wait at least five minutes before leaving. Turning the ignition off, she settled back in the high seat, adjusting the rearview mirror. "You did good, James, but keep alert," she whispered as she patted the dash of her car.

The cats remained surprisingly quiet. Matthey was grateful and unnerved. Gaffer and Cristo had never shown appropriate behaviour before. It crossed her mind to think about it. It also crossed her mind to think who was in the green car. However, her brain was jammed to the rafters with overactive adrenalin and she was, basically, incapable of thinking intelligently about anything. Any thoughts crossing her mind saw the "No Vacancy" sign and split.

When she had sat there long enough to be aware that her ear itched, she rolled down her window very slowly and listened. Dead silence slowly blended into the sounds of a night bird, a stereo playing a barely discernable Chopin etude, a helicopter circling over the freeway a few miles ahead and a dog barking.

Keeping her headlights off and taking a deep breath, Matthey started the engine. It sounded like a jackhammer pounding into steel. Slowly, she pulled forward, intending to go to the end of the next block and turn left. Within seconds a loud "gaflatta, gaflatta" reached Matthey's ears. At the same time she became aware it was impossible to steer. "Oh, God, I've got a flat tire," she exhaled.

A lower brain instinct made her roll up the window. The same instinct made her body break out in a sweat and her breathing become panting. The little guy in her brain had just jammed the stress lever full up. No street lights. Her phone was dead, she remembered. And some psycho is roaming the streets. She knew her tires had been in good shape. "Fight or flight, eh, Dr. Tom?"

Matthey was not anxious to get out of the car. She was equally not eager to sit there all night. The decision was taken out of her hands. Both cats began a low, guttural chirp when the three of them heard the tapping on the back-right window. Without looking, Matthey's hand locked onto the horn and held there. When her pulse slowed enough to allow her to glance around, she realized that lights had gone on in the surrounding houses. No one had come outside but several curtains were pulled aside to allow faces to stare into the darkness. She saw no one at her car window. Turning on the headlights she jumped out to stand in the beams. She yelled "call the police" loud enough to be confident someone heard it, then jumped back in the car and locked the door. She leaned on the horn again, just to make sure someone would call the cops if only to report a disturbance. It worked. The house lights remained on, the curtains stayed open and Officers Scorza and Flanningham arrived within four minutes.

They showed her where her rear, right tire had been slashed. They pointed out the flowers, just off the curb that were smashed and trampled. Matthey told them what had happened. They helped her put the spare on and she followed them to the Glendale police station to file a report. It didn't take long. She didn't have much to say. They said they would let her know if they found out anything. They also cautioned her about driving that late at night.

Matthey called Bill, who was asleep but sober. He offered to drive to the police station and follow her back to his house. She said, no, she was fine and would be there in twenty minutes. A car with one headlight stayed behind her on the freeway but did not get off at Bill's exit. The little guy in Matthey's brain slowly started to pull the lever back down.

Chapter Sixteen

Matthey sat in the fourteenth pew on the house left side of the First Sharon Baptist Church. Apparently, Christine's paternal grandfather had been born in the hills of Kentucky and her parents had stayed in the faith. There had been an oil spill from an overturned tanker truck on the 710 freeway and most of the Hopkins Theatre contingent had been several minutes late arriving in Long Beach for the services.

Matthey had called Jeci that morning to assure him that Alan had, of course, insisted upon canceling rehearsal in order for the cast to attend Christine's memorial. She didn't tell him about the four o'clock rehearsal that everyone was expected to return for. And she didn't tell him how pissed off Alan had been at the idea of losing rehearsal time. Or how he only became persuaded when Matthey brought up the press release that would be sent out mentioning Christine's death and Alan Davis' insistence that nothing should stand in the way of fellow performers paying tribute to a young artist. Alan, who lived in Santa Monica and came down the 405 was on time. He was sitting directly behind the grandparents in the third pew. Matthey had rushed in just minutes after they finally started the service, the minister being unable to wait any longer. A wedding was planned for four o'clock.

While the organist pounded and a chubby radiant teenager in purple satin sang about redemption, Matthey looked around. Gloria and her boyfriend were sitting over on the right, up a couple of pews. Gloria was in tears. Jason was sitting with other members of the cast just behind the two of them. Matthey was relieved to see that most of the company had turned up. Tony and Carole were back at the theatre ensuring the readiness of the stage for rehearsal. She had promised Alan. Annie and the other designers were taking advantage of the time to get some work done onstage. No sign of Che and Isabel but she didn't really expect them. They had never met Christine and would probably feel uncomfortable.

The minister rose from his chair to stand at the pulpit. He was an unpleasant looking man. Not ugly, but young enough to be so hideously bland as to be annoying. He looked at his watch as he set his notes on the podium. Matthey bet his children hated him and would grow up to be drug addicts.

Everyone stood up for the prayer. "Dear Lord of Lights, this time with you is for us and for all those we love, for those with us, and those who are now apart from us. In remembering our commitment to you and them and to Christine, make known to the world through us, their light, life and warmth, now and in the darkest hours. Amen." Everyone sat and reached for their copy of the Book of Common Prayer.

The preacher began a sermon concentrating on those who die in their youth. "Those whom the good Lord chooses to bring to his bosom while still in the first blossom of spring's awakening." The demulcent reverend began to warm to the notion of Christine spending her summers doing high dives for The Man in that big swimming pool in the sky. His innocuous cheeks became rosy. He became more animated and enthusiastic with a segue into a more personal evaluation of "the young deceased". Obviously enjoying the complete attention of the congregation, he began to talk about the sins of youth, and then, more specifically, the sins of Christine.

The "good die young" had no place in this preacher's philosophy. "Because every human being is full of sin" and, apparently, he felt Mr. and Mrs. Martinez' young daughter was no exception. In fact, everyone should be grateful that she was, right now, as he spoke, confessing all those horrible indiscretions to God and, once unburdened, joining the pure spirit of light. The minister was a man who relished sins and, once onto the subject, became almost blandly eloquent extolling the multitude of Christine's evil thoughts and deeds and the relief she must now be feeling having rid herself of them.

It was around this point that the maternal grandmother managed to extricate her arm from the firm grip of her son and struggle to her feet. Waving her cane and shouting a phrase in Spanish that could only be translated as hostile to the oblivious minister she pushed past her family and marched up the center aisle and exited the church. A young woman, possibly Christine's sister, hurried after her. As Matthey turned to watch them leave, she glimpsed Che and Isabel slipping out a side door. So, she thought, they had come after all. Well, that was nice, she supposed. She'd tell them so back at the theatre.

The minister, finally sensing his loss of popularity with the crowd, quickly summed up his sermon with a rendering of "The Lord's Prayer". Christine's brother read a tribute to her, the satin girl sang another song and the service was over.

As Matthey hurried outside, after saying a few words to Christine's parents and to Jeci, she barely avoided being run over by a navy-blue Chevrolet decorated with streamers and a sign saying "Just Married" on its bumper. Several girls in pastel coloured taffeta dresses were standing in a group checking their make-up in pocket mirrors. When Matthey reached her car, she was surprised to find she was crying so hard she had trouble finding the lock with the key. Embarrassed at her confusion she hurriedly put her sunglasses on, jammed The New World Symphony in the CD hole and sang along at the top of her lungs on her ride back to the theatre. There was traffic. This was Los Angeles, after all.

96

Detective Mally was waiting for her in her office when she walked in. So was Che. They seemed to be having a pleasant conversation. Each looked quite relaxed. Apparently, the policeman had also been at the services. However, he had stayed in his car outside. His partner had been inside among the mourners. When Che and Isabel left, Mally had followed them back to the theatre. He told this to Matthey after Che had excused himself. Seems Che was using the phone when Mally walked in the office. He identified himself as a policeman investigating the stolen car and had a friendly chat with Che about his involvement with the play and this led into a discussion about regional theatre and its place in the country. The way Mally told it, he came across as a regular Colombo. Matthey doubted that Che had been fooled for an instant. But she smiled at the cop and decided to tell him about the incident driving last night.

Matthey had once applied to the Los Angeles police department a few years back when her career had seemed stagnant. Her interview had consisted of two questions dealing with "if you were in this situation what-would-you-do?" She had calmly and concisely explained every conceivable scenario that might arise if this, or this, or that, or, of course, this were a motivating factor and too late she noticed the glazed eyes of her questioners and realized that they only wanted the simple, obvious, single course of action, not the endless possibilities. Many months later she was notified that she had passed, barely, and could now apply for the next level, the physical. Her career had become a bit more interesting at this point and she filed the form letter and thought about it now and then. She was sure Mally had done well with his interview.

"So, I have no idea if there's any connection, but I figured I should let you know what happened, since you're here and all," Matthey said, finishing up her account of the episode. She sat at the

97

desk. She didn't care that he was sitting in the chair. The phone rang. When she picked it up it reeked of English Leather. She forgot to say hello for a second.

"Hello, it's Che. I know the policeman was there on official business, so I didn't want to annoy you. I'm afraid Isabel won't be able to be at the rehearsal this afternoon. She became very ill suddenly at the church."

"God, Che, what's wrong with her?"

"I wouldn't worry. It's just a little stomach thing. I'm confident Isabel will be fine tomorrow."

"Uh, how about the show tonight? If she's not that sick, it's, uh, kind of a theatre tradition that you rise above it and go on anyway."

"I believed you would be concerned that her illness might be passed to another member of the cast. We were trying to be considerate of the others."

Matthey looked through the mirror at Mally. He was staring at her and made no attempt to avert his eyes. He wasn't writing. Matthey sighed.

"Well, Che, infecting the company is certainly a consideration, however, if everyone felt that way, we'd always have understudies on and would probably be cancelling shows because the understudies would be out, too. Actors are always sick. So are the crew. It's something about theatre. It encourages bacteria and viruses. People in theatre love to get sick and come to work and complain about how sick they are. It's essential to the artistic spirit. There is an exception to this rule, however. Stage managers. Stage managers never get sick. Ever. And, if by some miracle, one of us does become ill, we never talk about it. Why, you might ask, if you were interested, which you're not. And that's why. You're not interested. No one

98

cares if the stage manager is sick because it makes them uneasy. When a child is seven and wants Daddy to play and Daddy says 'I can't right now, honey, I'm not feeling well' the child doesn't care. The child isn't concerned, he just wants Daddy to play and is miffed when he doesn't. And, so it is with the stage manager. We don't get sick because no one will be concerned when we do. In fact, our fellow employees of the theatre--the actors, stagehands, managers, designers, office staff tend to get downright miffed if we should happen to mention we're not in the best of shape. Well, enough about me. Che, I hope to see Isabel tonight. Please tell her we all hope she feels better. Call me before half hour and let me know how she's doing. I'd call you but I still don't have a phone number. It's been swell talking to you. Bye."

Matthey hung up the phone and swirled around to face Mally. He had, what only a loving mother might describe as, a smile on his face. It could, by a small stretch of the imagination, be described as a smug smile.

"Yes?" Matthey asked.

"It hasn't been a good day, has it, Ms. Cole?"

"Oh, was I that rude to him?" Matthey got her templet out of her notebook and stuck a pencil through the 5/16" hole and started twirling.

"No, you weren't. But I've seen you more equanimous. And your eyes are red. And you couldn't have had much sleep last night."

"Guilty. But not complaining."

"Who do you think was in the car last night?"

"I have no idea. Some asshole looking for some kicks."

"Yesterday, you told me you assumed the person who hit Christine was some joyrider, nothing intentional. Now you say the guy who may have been trying to seriously hurt you is just some wierdo who happened to see you, could have been anyone. Have you always had such a haphazard view of life?"

"Plot is a creation of writers and undertakers. God created chance, Officer Mally. Flexibility and a car with a full tank of gas is what I believe in. Now what can I do for you?" Matthey reversed the direction of the spin of the templet.

The policeman looked at her. "Keep your eyes and ears open. Be careful. Somebody wants something and I want to know who and what before somebody else gets hurt. How well do you know this Che and Isabel?"

It was Matthey's turn to look at Mally. "Just a couple of days. She doesn't speak English very well and Che takes care of her."

"They have green cards?"

"I've seen hers. We're not paying him so it hasn't been an issue."

"You have no phone number or address for them?"

"Apparently, they're in the process of moving and are staying at different places until they get settled."

"Does that seem unusual to you?"

Matthey stopped twirling and leaned back. "Detective Mally, I have worked in many theatres for many years. I've had an actor gunned down by hit men and I've organized blood donations and protection shifts for him. I've had an actor tell me she's had an abortion and was worried that she might start bleeding during the performance and have to leave. She was nude throughout the show. I made sure she had plenty of tampax. I've arrived at the theatre to discover my platform set had been rearranged as a banquet table with white vinyl staple-gunned around all the units and food crumbs everywhere. I've had to sort out the problems resulting from every conceivable in-house sexual coupling. I've had actors demand we ask the audience to stop coughing or they won't go on. I've stopped shows because of people dying in the house. I've stood with the house manager as we waited to see if a bomb threat would be actualized since management decided not to inform anyone of it. I've taken over the light board from a drunken operator who flipped out because his father wasn't proud of him. I've watched designers have nervous breakdowns and never show up again. I've worked on plays that only an idiot would produce and I've watched beautiful writing be bastardized by dramaturgs and directors who have convinced themselves that commercialism is really art. No, Detective Mally, it does not seem unusual to me. It seems no more than what it is. Excuse me, but I have a rehearsal starting momentarily and I have a million things to do. Is there anything else?"

"No. Not now. But please call me if you have any more trouble." He stood and started to walk out. "Oh, and I hope you'll go straight home tonight and get some sleep. Good-by."

Matthey heard him go through the stage door. "What home? Which set of keys is home? Even my suitcases are borrowed." Matthey stared at herself in the mirror and watched a tear leak out of her right eye. That will not do, she thought. No, that will not do at all. Quite unforgivable. Back to work, my dear.

And, twirling her templet, she went onstage to check with Tony and Carole.

Chapter Seventeen

101

Alan arrived back at the theatre by a quarter after four and spent half an hour passionately discoursing about the theatrical quality of the memorial service. He felt the grandmother was a hero of epic proportions and "you must understand that Louis' whole catharsis depends upon you being imbued with that same sense of prideful mourning, that almost arrogant grief, when Jacques dies."

The cast then began exchanging stories about their funereal experiences. Jason's father was an undertaker in Iowa and he had a wonderful story about his second grade teacher, Mrs. Duncan, being laid out in his living room for viewing and him being terrified and eventually realizing she couldn't hurt him and him opening the lid and poking her and sticking his tongue out at her and calling her names and getting carried away until the school principal walked in to pay his respects and caught him and made him stay there while the teacher's husband came in and looked at his wife with loathing and Jason remembered the book she had given him about this little boy who lives with his evil grandfather but learns to imagine himself in the most wonderful locations and grows up and moves to New York and becomes a famous actor, and she'd given him this book for no reason, just as a present, and after the husband and principal left he went and kissed her on the cheek and promised her she'd love New York.

Listening to him, Matthey noticed a distinctly unusual pallor to his face that she had never noticed before. She thought Jason might be more interesting than had previously occurred to her.

Since the majority of actors like to talk more than they like to rehearse, and Alan was encouraging them no actual rehearsal took place. But the show that night was wonderful, and Alan didn't give any notes necessitating any major changes. Che showed up with Isabel. She was quiet but did her role and they stayed in the correct dressing rooms. They left as soon as notes were over, and Matthey found herself heading to the valley before midnight. She was still driving on the spare, one of those small, over-inflated tires that the new cars used, and she cursed her need to keep her speed down.

Matthey got to Bill's house just minutes before he arrived home from work. He had spent the day taping a Christmas special with Lionel Richie, Donna Summer, Fawn Hall and the Cabbage Patch Doll Choir. Bill said it had some cute things in it even if it was awfully dated. It gave him enough money to invest in another house, his fifth. He played with Brady for a few minutes, put the trash cans out on the street then went into the kitchen to pour some vodka into a glass. Matthey already had a beer but followed him in. She had smelled liquor on him when he kissed her hello.

"You look tired. How did the show go?" She reached into the cabinet behind her and handed him a glass.

"It went well. Nothing special. Lionel Richie does one terrific number, though. Ed Marito did the choreography. Oh, and Beth Hunter says hello."

"Oh, Beth was one of the dancers, eh?" Both Ed and Beth had been on the Jesus Christ, Superstar tour that she had met Bill on. "Do you have to work tomorrow?"

"Let me have some of those cashews." Matthey reached behind her to open the glass cabinet. She poured the nuts from the Taster's Choice jar into his hand. "I have a meeting at eight for the "Del Winters Awards Show", one at nine for the Chevy industrial, one at ten for the "Comedy Spot." We're taping a "Where are the Stars" tomorrow and I have a meeting at six with the architect for the Spring house."

"You're going to do that addition to the garage?"

"Have to. A one car garage and two-bedroom house in that neighbourhood will never have any resale. Come on Brady, let's go in the living room."

Matthey followed behind the prancing dog and wondered if Bill was going to drink himself into a stupor. He didn't seem to mind her sudden semi-permanent presence in the house, but he hadn't expressed any enjoyment of it either. Bill threw some pillows on the floor and settled himself, stomach down, on top of them. Brady snuggled in by his side. Using the remote he turned on the television. He flipped through the channels and settled on a rerun of "LA Law". Matthey had grown to loathe the show.

She stood with her back to the fireplace. Stacks of magazines filled up the inside. A black tail feathered across her cheek as Cristo crossed the top of the mantle to settle down in the alcove on the right. Gaffer was lying down on the left side, but alert. Although Brady had finally remembered he wasn't welcome as their companion Gaffer did not yet trust him. Bill pulled the newspaper over and opened it to the crossword puzzle.

Matthey said, "I had a few words with Joe Murphy again." Joe was the house carpenter at the Hopkins. Bill and he had worked together, many years earlier, in New York. "He was pissed off that I made the crew come in for the rehearsal and then Alan and the cast spent the whole time sitting onstage talking. He was much friendlier after dinner, but I suspect that was a couple of brandies talking."

Bill filled in the answer to one across. "Don't be too hard on Joe. I understand him pretty well. Being in show business for a long time can be hard. Especially on those who are the brightest."

Matthey became excited at Bill's apparent willingness to carry on a conversation. She also realized how rather pathetic her excitement was. "What an interesting comment. Are you speaking about everyone, in general, or just technicians?"

"I'm not a technician." Bill shifted so he faced away from her. Brady adjusted accordingly.

"I didn't say you were. But it is your background and a large part of the people you deal with are stagehands. And most of your closest friends are in the union."

Bill sighed. "Is Jerry Kruger in I.A.T.S.E.?" Jerry was a stockbroker who had met Bill a few years ago when he advised him on an investment. He was the brother of an old girlfriend and they had retained a good friendship.

Matthey sighed. "OK. Right. Jerry. But how about Bobby and Jimmy and Benny and Timmy and Lucas?" She thought to herself, I guess even the IA couldn't stomach calling him Lukey.

Bill got up to pour himself another drink. This time he filled the glass.

Matthey used the opportunity to get another beer. "So, you were speaking generally, then." Bill didn't say anything. "Then, that's fascinating. Here, one would think that show business would be considered a creative stimulant, bringing out the best of people's minds, provoking those in its ranks to be continually challenged by new ideas. We're always changing jobs. Every show means new problems, new personalities, different ways of looking at things. Every time I do a play, I find something in the script to enlighten me. Even a bad play. Well, not always a bad play. Sometimes they just suck, but usually it's like reading a good book, except in theatre I feel a part of the creation. That final outcome on the stage, in front of a paying audience, owes something, no matter how small, to me--to my talents. I think that's rather wonderful."

Matthey smiled at herself for being right and for ignoring Bill's reticence to continue upholding his end of the dialogue. Bill had settled back on the pillows.

"Matthey, if you weren't doing it, someone else would be and the show would still be opening on the same night to the same paying audience. Your presence doesn't change a thing."

"Yes, yes, of course, it still would open but that doesn't mean anything."

"I thought it did."

"I mean, it wouldn't be exactly the same play. There might be a line missing that I would have persuaded the playwright to keep in. The way the lights are called with the sound wouldn't have exactly the same rhythms. When an understudy goes on, he won't have the same understanding that I would have given him. Or it may not even be the same understudy that I would have encouraged hiring. The psychological mood of the rehearsal process and backstage won't have the same ambience that I would have brought to it. Tempers might fly that wouldn't have had I been there. Tempers that affect the performance. I might have persuaded an actor not to quit who was frustrated or prevented the director from firing one. Or my encouragement may have resulted in a few chances being taken and my disapproval may have saved money being spent on yet another change of mind. The music we're using in Amazon Loophole was my suggestion. The director's decision but my idea. If I hadn't been involved, he wouldn't have had it to consider."

Bill filled in fourteen down. "To Joe, Amazon Loophole is just a set similar to a lot of other sets with the usual asshole allotment of actors, directors and designers. No one cares what he thinks of the show or how he might improve on it. Probably, nobody even knows his name yet, certainly not his last name. Nobody cares that he may have a couple of plays that he's written which are hidden in a desk drawer that he's never shown to anyone. Maybe a poem or two. All people see is a coarse carpenter with dirty fingernails and they wouldn't see anything else even if you told them different. Even if he offered the most insightful contribution to the script he'd be smiled at, patronized and ignored. The only thing about Joe that anyone takes notice of is his salary. Everyone gets pissed off that he and the crew make more than anyone else."

"Well, it's difficult for a lot of people to rationalize paying people so much money when they do tend to sit around a lot. I know Joe has worked incredibly hard putting the show into the theatre and keeping up with the changes these past couple of weeks, but he also gets an incredible amount of overtime for that. And once we open and stop rehearsing, he and Jay will alternate coming in to do the set up but they'll both still get full salaries."

Bill erased one of his words in the puzzle and stared at the empty space.

Matthey continued "I think Joe's angry because he went to college to study history but got sucked into the union because his father was a member and it required no education and he was young and the money was enough to buy a house before he was twenty-three and the girls loved riding in his sports car and spending weekends in the Bahamas. How do you give that up to struggle as a history teacher?"

Bill refilled the empty space and lettered in two others. "I didn't know Joe wanted to be a history teacher."

"He mentioned it once, very casually. I don't know if he was serious. He had his first kid when he was twenty-four and now, two divorces and three kids later he probably has to stay on top of a few bills. I think he's angry because he knows he settled for less than he could have been."

"And he did, darlin'. So, did we all. Everybody gets into this business secretly wanting to be a star. To be big and powerful and important. Be noticed, stand out, be unique." Bill didn't actually turn to face her, but he shifted his weight so that his body now angled toward her. Brady got up and moved around to the other side of Bill so he could resume snuggling into Bill's stomach.

Bill continued concentrating on the puzzle. "Most of them settle for being able to order production assistants around. When the money starts coming in, which it usually does, if you're lucky and talented, and if you haven't gotten discouraged, then you're stuck. Oh, you might have dreams of doing something worthwhile, of taking a chance but all that money keeps you complacent. It becomes your pimp. You'll whore for it, work on any piece of dreck just to keep the illusion that you've succeeded in becoming a star. And, in those hours of the day and night where everywhere you look you see your own reflection, you learn to close off part of you, the part that's filled with yearning. Drugs, alcohol, self-denial, whatever works. Convince yourself that money's the only important thing, bottom line. What you make is what you're worth."

"You don't think that the guy selling shirts at Sears in St. Louis doesn't have dreams of grandeur?"

"Maybe he does, darlin', but he didn't act on them. We did. Everybody who actually made the attempt to go for the gold in this business believed, somewhere in their gut, that, initially, they had a chance. This business is filled with failed megalomaniacs from the chairman of MGM who thought he'd produce the movie that would make Citizen Kane seem sophomoric and instead found himself sucking up to corporate money and making movies about teenage nerds because they kept him in his job. He's no different from the make-up man who dreamed of being helicoptered to locations because only he could make this or that star look the way they wanted, but, instead, took this job on a soap and he works every day and they like him so he know he's got a long gig with a good income that means he can plan for a few things and his family is thrilled that he's working with the daytime stars but he knows that his dreams have just ended and why refuse a line of cocaine that this actor just offered him."

"So, then, of course, the soap actor feels the same."

"That's right, darlin'."

"Then you're saying it's better not to go after your dreams. Have them but make no attempt to act on them because you'll only be disappointed in yourself when you settle for less."

"I'm not saying anything. I'm just talking." Bill had finished his drink and was resting his head on the floor. The crossword puzzle was almost done.

"I don't feel I've settled."

"Didn't you start off wanting to be a movie star?"

"Yes, but that was when I was younger, and once I realized that I wanted to live <u>in</u> an adventure movie not act in one I stopped wanting to perform. I haven't had any desire along those lines for at least fifteen years."

"You don't want your bio in the program or your name on the posters or the playwright to announce to all that your influence was crucial to the success of his play? You don't want an actor to accept a Tony and thank you for the encouragement and support you've given him? You don't secretly think, given the right situation, you could out-act, out-direct, out-write, out-produce everyone you work with?"

Matthey grimaced. "Well, at least I never thought I could out-design anyone." Her hand idly scratched Cristo's rear end. "I suppose you have a point, but I don't know that I like it. From a personal standpoint, I mean. Settling implies fear to me. And I've always been terrified of being a fearful person." She watched Bill lie on the floor, one arm now around Brady.

"What about you? Do you feel you've settled? How do you deal with that? What yearning have you compromised? Bill?"

Bill answered her by beginning to snore. Hesitant sounds with no rhythm. Matthey sighed and felt her body deflating. She looked down on the sleeping form with tenderness and anger.

"I love you, Bill. I really do. It amazes me that I can be certain of anything, but I am certain I love you. I guess, I thank you for that."

She looked at the remaining beer in her glass and swallowed it in one gulp. "But, darlin', I'm just not certain that loving you means one whole hell of a lot."

Matthey took a few minutes to clean up. After washing her face and brushing her teeth she managed to get Bill into bed without too much difficulty. They fell asleep with his arm pulling her into him and his lips on her back.

Chapter Eighteen

The next morning Matthey called Debbie to let her know she didn't know anything. She told her about Mally believing Christine's death wasn't an accident and she mentioned her own driving incident. She didn't mention that she thought Isabel was one of the coldest people she'd ever met. She did say, however, that Isabel was doing a nice job in her group scene. "And no, I can't tell if she's talented. There won't be an understudy rehearsal until after we open."

Debbie was quite excited and was sure it was all related and cautioned Matthey to be careful. Matthey assured her she would and promised to get back to her soon. Debbie said she was going to be unreachable for two days because of one of her top-secret things but she'd be back in the office on Monday. The second Matthey replaced the receiver on the phone it rang. It was Che.

"Matthey, hello. I hoped I would find you at home before leaving for the theatre."

"Has Isabel become worse? I can recommend doctors."

"No, she seems fine, now. There is no problem. I have an address and telephone number to give you. I believe you were anxious to receive them."

"Yes, that's great. What are they?" Matthey dug in her purse for a pencil and using the back of a receipt that was laying on Bill's desk she wrote down the information. "Thanks, Che. I'll try to type up a new contact list this afternoon."

"Don't you have it on a computer?"

"Well, yes and no. I use Pages and everyone else uses Word and I've transferred it to Word but screwed up and it became a PDF instead so I can't change it or at least I can't figure out how to change it so it's just easier to retype everything and get it right this time. Sounds pretty low tech, eh?"

"Rather inefficient. I'm surprised. You appear very organized. I would assume you value your time more than that."

"Yeah, well, I value my time enough to want to experience it, not just program it."

"I'm not sure I understand."

"Neither am I. It's not important. Is there anything else you need?" Like help taking a shower, she thought. Stop thinking like that! Right! "I don't think rehearsal will last the full five hours today. Alan was very happy with the show last night and has very few notes. And the photo calls usually go relatively quickly."

"That is wonderful. I was hoping you would be able to join me for dinner. There are a couple of details I would like to discuss with you. Are you available?"

Matthey blew her hair out of her eyes. "More than likely I'll be free. There's always the chance that something will develop in rehearsal that means I have to work through dinner, but I imagine I'll have the time."

"Then I will speak to you later at the theatre and we'll make arrangements."

"Fine. See you later." Matthey hung up and debated calling Debbie back. She decided she might as well wait until after the dinner. She had no intention of having work to do.

She quickly showered and drank her protein drink. Brady and Cristo followed her from room to room and Gaffer stretched out on the back of the couch blinking in the sunlight. Bill called to ask if she'd put the garbage cans away. He'd forgotten. Once outside, she decided to walk around the corner to the 7-ll to buy juice and milk. She also bought a bunch of tulips and put them in a vase on the living room table. After checking to make sure all the water dishes were filled with fresh water she drove to the theatre. She had meant to buy a new tire, but two cars were in line at the tire store and she didn't have time to wait.

Rehearsal proved to be relatively low key. There had been no tech notes so most of the crew wasn't called until the photo call at 3:30pm. Alan was still in a good mood. The rewrites were all minor ones. A line or word here and there. There was no problem stopping at three for half hour and the photo call lasted the promised thirty minutes. Matthey and Alan spent another forty-five minutes rehearsing two scene changes and by five o'clock everyone was ready to leave. Matthey told Che she'd be ready in five minutes and he said he'd get the car and meet her outside.

Tony caught her just as she was grabbing her purse and coat. "Did Gloria talk to you?"

"No, why? Is there a problem?"

"I don't know. But when she came in, she asked where you were, and I said you were across the street going over the photo call with the press department. She said fine, she'd catch you later. She had a funny expression on her face, though. It kind of worried me."

"She never said a word during the rehearsal or the photo call."

"Well, you know Gloria. Once she gets into the play it's her sole focus. But I think you should talk to her."

Matthey put her coat on. "Oh, I will. As soon as I get back from dinner. Thanks for telling me. Oh, Tony, I put Isabel's new phone number on the mirror there. Finally, eh? Che called me this morning with it. See you later."

She was surprised to discover that Isabel wasn't with Che as he opened the front car door for her. She wasn't surprised to see he was driving a white Mercedes Benz 280 SL.

"Where did you have in mind going for dinner?" she asked, watching him as he very cautiously pulled into the street traffic.

"Isabel felt she should rest between the rehearsal and the show. She's still a little tired and she's promised to take a nap over dinner."

"Oh, well, that's probably a good idea. She did seem a little pale today." Matthey's lips suddenly felt dry and she dug some lip balm from her purse. She applied it as Che passed by the freeway exits and headed toward Sunset Blvd. She assumed he was heading toward one of the numerous Mexican restaurants on that end of Sunset. "How is her English coming? I really haven't spoken to Isabel much, I'm afraid."

"Isabel is very shy. She has all her dialogue memorized and is prepared to go on at any time. She is very good." He crossed Sunset and started winding up toward the hills above Silverlake.

"If she is so shy then I imagine she's going to have trouble with the nudity. 'Danais' has no self-consciousness about her body. She's completely innocent about the men's awareness of her sexuality. If Isabel should ever go on, she'll be jumping cold into the nudity in front of seven hundred people. If there's any evidence of her being uncomfortable the play goes out the window."

The Mercedes turned right onto a small street going further uphill. "Isabel has a beautiful body. She will have no trouble. There is no need to be concerned."

"I'm sure she does but if there's even a hint of self-consciousness this piece loses its validity."

"It is not a problem. Please, we do not need to discuss this further." Matthey made a mental note to talk to Alan about Isabel.

The road turned into dirt and Che downshifted into second. Rounding a curve Matthey was surprised to find they were on the side of the hill with an unobstructed overview of downtown Los Angeles. She could even see the top of the Hopkins peeking around the Bank of

America. Matthey had a sudden fantasy of Che kidnapping her, shooting her full of heroin and forcing her into unspeakable acts while Isabel stars on Broadway and wins Tony after Tony. What one had to do with the other wasn't clear, but her gut felt the relation.

Che made a left into a driveway that adjoined a small, white Spanish style bungalow with a decidedly modern influence. The front yard was terraced and was filled with plants and flowers in a somewhat chaotic pattern. It reminded Matthey of the gardens of Aranjuez, outside Madrid. Wild and brooding. She had been mesmerized there, one overcast afternoon. Even in the sunlight of Los Angeles the front yard seemed to be in the shadows though there wasn't a cloud in the sky.

She realized this was probably the address that Che had given her. Bushes and trees overwhelmed the sides and back of the home, but the front was open to the garden and the view. Matthey tried to understand what the feeling in the pit of her stomach was signifying. She followed Che up the stone walk to the front door and wondered why she wasn't asking why they were here.

"I thought it would be more comfortable if we had our dinner here," Che said, leading her into the living room. "It's so much more convenient than a noisy restaurant and I'm afraid I must be careful with my finances at the moment. I'm expecting some money fairly soon and I don't wish to over-due before it arrives." Che indicated Matthey should sit on the couch and he went behind a black slate bar and opened a bottle of red wine.

Matthey tried to breathe normally as she seated herself in the off-white overly cushioned sofa. She wondered if it was stuffed with down as she felt herself sink into it.

"How do you and Isabel know each other? Are you acquainted with her family?"

He poured the wine generously into two large ceramic goblets. "Her uncle and I had some business dealings once. I joined the family for dinner and met Isabel and her aunt, my friend's wife."

"And her father? Did you meet him as well?" She took the glass of wine from Che and watched him as he settled into a contrasting chair across from her. He was wearing an off-white linen suit with a mauve tee-shirt underneath and a silver belt. It couldn't be more cliché. However, clichés become so because, originally, they were so striking that they were envied and emulated. Che had an ability to revalidate a cliché. Matthey's lower anatomy was doing some sort of rain dance that only it understood. She felt her eyes hood over slightly. She thought of Dr. Tom. Her lower brain was asserting itself.

"Her father died when Isabel was born. He had no family. It was an arranged marriage. Isabel's mother did not mourn very deeply."

"Isabel has some very Anglo features. I just wondered if there was any mixture there?" Matthey hoped her attempt to be subtle didn't come across as racist

"Perhaps. I never met the father. Or perhaps an ancestor further back. It does not interest me. I promised Isabel's uncle and aunt that I would help her get settled in Los Angeles. They are naturally hoping she will be successful as an actress. I am confident she will be. I am fortunate to know several people here and I believe her talent will be recognized quickly." Che got up to pour Matthey more wine. She was embarrassed to realize that she had finished her glass while his sat untouched.

"What is it that you do, Che? I take it you're more than just a manager. Do you have any interest in acting, yourself?"

Che put the bottle on the table. "Please forgive me, I've not offered you any food. One moment, please."

He disappeared around the corner of the bar and Matthey heard a refrigerator open and close. While she waited and sipped on the burgundy the room was suddenly filled with a compact disc recording of something that sounded like Latin jazz fused with a rock beat. Che appeared holding a plate of hors d'oeuvres. He sat next to her as he placed the plate on the table in front of them.

They looked like some kind of soft cheese wrapped in a thin slice of raw fish. The second glass of wine and the syncopated four/four rhythm were making the water content of Matthey's body feel like it had just gotten back onto land after being on a boat for a week. The gentle undulation was both lulling and alarming. Che picked up one of the appetizers.

"I had these once in Seville. It's very difficult to find just the right cheese with the consistency and the sharpness. I was fortunate. Los Angeles is filled with such a variety of food stores."

Matthey reached for one of the rose-coloured balls. Che stopped her, picking one up first and holding it to her mouth. She started to feel warm. Reaching out she took the food from his fingers with her mouth. Without thinking, her tongue darted out to catch a piece of cheese that stuck to the tip of his middle finger. She chewed, thinking that there were bits of pistachio in there. It was delicious. The inside of her mouth felt alive with the different sensations of the wine-sweetened cheese, the cold, smooth, slightly salty white fish and the hard nuts. There was another flavour she couldn't put her finger on.

"Please, now you give me one. It is a tradition to start a meal." Matthey had spent a month in Spain and had never heard of this tradition, but it didn't seem all that important to argue about.

Reaching down she picked the biggest one and held it to Che's lips. He looked at her a moment and then brought his left hand up to her wrist and gently held it in place as he slowly removed the morsel from her fingers, licking the tips in the process. Matthey started to remove her hand but felt the resistance from his other hand and held it there. The music was throbbing and so was her pulse. Very carefully Che brought her hand closer to his lips and inserted her forefinger between his lips and began to suck. Matthey felt the view closing in on her.

What seemed like hours later, he removed it from his mouth and inserted the next finger. As he slowly withdrew her from his mouth, she realized that his left hand no longer held hers but was offering her another hors d'oeuvre. She took it and his finger as it lingered there, wanting. Her eyes closed. She suckled and would have purred if she could.

Gently, Che removed his finger and she opened her mouth expecting the next finger. Instead his hand went behind her neck and pulled her to him. Her mouth was still anticipating when it met his and her arms wrapped around his neck with no hesitation. As their mouths exploded into one another she realized the elusive taste was marzipan and she reveled in it.

His left hand began to attend to the buttons on her sweater and she shifted slightly to make it easier. His hair felt incredible in her hands as she gripped it with her fingers while their mouths continued to ravage each other's. Che opened her sweater and pulled her tee-shirt free from her pants. Reaching up he covered her breast with his hand, gripping a nipple between two fingers and squeezing just enough to send ripples through her body. He adjusted her slightly and pulled off the sweater.

Moving the tee-shirt up to her neck he removed his mouth from hers and began sucking and biting her breasts. As her head rolled back, he pulled the tee-shirt over and tossed it behind the couch. All she could do was pull his shirt from his waistband and run her hands over his bare back. The skin was like a baby's. Che sat up and took his jacket off, throwing it over the back of the couch as well. He shifted Matthey so she was lying on the couch and looked at her as she ran her hands under his shirt and over his chest. "You're so beautiful, so very beautiful," he said while his fingers traced lines on her chest. Matthey quietly kicked off her shoes behind him.

"I want to see you naked," he said as his mouth went to her right nipple while his left hand reached down to unbutton her jeans. She lifted her ass to allow him to pull the pants down and off. She worked her socks off with her feet and lay there unable to touch more than his back. His right hand rested on her stomach while his left fingers roamed under the elastic of her underpants. Matthey moaned and arched her back, watching fireworks on the inside of her eyelids.

It felt like multitudes of wonderful, soft little creatures were probing into every hidden part of her. She couldn't move and she couldn't stop her body from undulating. She opened her eyes when she felt Che rip her underwear from her. There goes ten bucks, she thought somewhere in the recesses of her upper brain. Her lower brain was filled with pure sensation.

She closed her eyes again as Che's mouth insinuated itself in the imprint of her underwear. When one hand reached up to squeeze her nipple and the other inserted two fingers into her vagina she lost all awareness of her surroundings and, purring like she was born to it, ascended into an explosion of all the pieces of a complete rainbow in a cumulus nimbus sky.

Chapter Nineteen

Matthey awoke with the proverbial start. Che lay on top of her, his tee-shirt on but bare-assed. They were still connected. His breath felt sweet against her neck. She looked at her watch. An hour had passed since their arrival at the house. Plenty of time to get back to the theatre but no time to have dinner. If there had ever been a dinner to have. She looked over at the plate of hors d'oeuvres and felt ravenous. Stretching out her arm she managed to pull the plate over close enough to pick up one of the balls. She tried to chew without moving her jaw so she wouldn't wake Che. It wasn't easy and inhibited her enjoyment of the food. When she started on the second piece he moaned and opened her eyes.

"Mi Ifgt ubuk ttetre," Matthey stated eloquently, trying to swallow the food without sharing the visuals with Che. Instead of answering, Che's mouth closed on her right nipple and she felt him swelling inside her. She moaned before she could stop herself. Oh well, she thought, at least it's the right time of the month. Other more ominous thoughts crossed her mind before she surrendered her intellect to the more immediate and pressing desire that was overwhelming her. Ah, lust. The common denominator of us all. Once again, Matthey stopped thinking.

Twenty minutes later she and Che were pulling out of the driveway onto the dirt road. She was grateful for the bucket seats.

"Che, that was a wonderful, uh, dinner and, god knows, I needed it but it's really not such a good idea for us to get together again. Partially because of our working relationship and because I do have someone I'm involved with. I'm even living with him at the moment and I just wouldn't feel comfortable sneaking around everyone right now and with the show still in previews it's just not a good time, you understand?"

Che glanced at her for an instant. His dark glasses made it impossible for her to see his eyes. The hills and the clutch made it impossible for him to rest his hand on her.

"Matthey, it is obvious to me that this other man is not good for you. A lover as natural as you should never be neglected. But that is your decision. If you wish, this afternoon is already forgotten. It will be no more than a gleam in my eye when I see you or hear your name." There might have been something resembling an upturned mouth expression on his face.

Matthey smiled back at him. "Thank you." Agreed awfully easily, old boy, she thought. Either you do this a lot, something I don't want to think about, or you're not being totally honest with me. What a ridiculous thought! Of course, he's not, I'm hardly being honest with him. I think if everyone was totally honest with each other the need for thought would never have evolved. God, sex is great! Matthey decided not to raise any questions concerning the nature of Che's interest in Isabel. It could only lead to complications if she expressed curiosity. There was a tiny niggling of guilt hinting at a betrayal of her relationship with Debbie but, hell, Debbie wouldn't really care, and she'd never met Ben, the husband, anyway, never even seen a picture. Matthey wasn't really concerned about Bill at all. One would have to stretch the imagination to claim she had cheated on him. She suspected that Bill might even agree with her on that.

Che was turning off Sunset onto the street leading up to the side of the Hopkins. So, back to work. It was good that Alan hadn't changed much of the show today. It would give the cast a chance to really sink their teeth into the play tonight, instead of just trying to remember what was new. Tonight, was an important performance. Two different producers from the Shubert organization were coming to look at the show for a possible future Broadway production. The Hopkins had wanted them to wait until after opening but they both had other New York shows going into previews in a few days which they had to oversee. Tonight coincided with a three day conference on the importance of Broadway to regional theatre, funded by AT&T, an important source to cultivate for investments. The conference was being hosted by the Los Angeles Theatre Collaborative, another regional theatre. The Shuberts were also interested in a Collaborative production that had opened to rave reviews last week and in a show in San Diego that was opening tomorrow.

"Matthey, you have been very quiet. I hope I haven't upset you?" Che pulled into the turnaround and faced her, letting the car idle.

"No, no, no. I'm sorry. I was just thinking about the show. You know, there's always something that needs to get done."

"Such as?"

"Oh, you know, something. I don't know." None of the cast knew the importance of tonight. No point in making them any more anxious than they already were. They knew this show had more of a potential than most.

"Listen, uh, thanks, I guess. Darn good dinner. Sorry, I have to run but I'm a bit later than I usually am. I mean I know it's well before half hour, but I usually get back earlier than this. Are you coming in?"

"No, I shall attend to a few errands and then come back. If you see Isabel, please tell her I'll be back before the show starts."

He picked up her hand and held the palm to his lips. A definite half smile flickered across his face. For a few seconds Matthey felt things blur again as she looked into his eyes. Or tried to. A loud rap on the window brought her to her senses.

"Matthey, my God, where have you been? Everybody's been looking for you." Edward, the head usher and close friend of George stood outside the car, a look of great excitement glowing from him. Matthey started to roll down the window, realized it was electric and went to open the door instead. But Che needed to electrically unlock it so she ended up pushing the lever that lowered the window.

"Edward, what's the matter?"

"I'm not exactly sure, but everyone's running around backstage screaming where's Matthey? I must have had at least fifty people want to know if I've seen you. Something to do with someone hurt, I think."

Matthey looked back at Che who still stared at her with the half smile and electric black lenses. Without taking his eyes off her he reached back with his left hand and pushed the button that unlocked the door.

"See you later," she heard as she opened and closed the Mercedes door. She broke into a run toward the stage door of the Hopkins.

Chapter Twenty

Matthey pushed her way through the door with dread and guilt combining in her body creating that awful sinking feeling that invades when one realizes something terrible has happened and you intuitively know your actions have somehow enabled it all to occur. She instinctively ran toward Gloria's dressing room. Rounding the corner, she stopped abruptly at the sight of Carole lying on the floor with half of her skull bashed in. Lying next to her was a twenty-pound stage weight. As Matthey heard the siren in the distance, she saw that both the weight and Carole's head were swimming in a large dark puddle of blood. They weren't doing the breaststroke. Carole's open and blank eyes left no doubt that she and the weight had one more thing in common--no living gray matter. Aw shit, was what Matthey said to herself. "What happened" was what she asked the subdued group of people standing around Carole.

"Tony found her," said Jason. Matthey glanced at him and realized he was the only one who didn't look particularly horrified. Of course, she thought, he's seen much worse in his living room back in Iowa. He's probably already decided the best way to reconstruct for the family viewing. She looked at Tony.

"I was coming down from upstairs and heard the phone ringing in the office and raced around the corner and almost tripped over her. I didn't hear a thing. Of course, I was in the bathroom so probably I wouldn't. But she wasn't there when I went up five minutes before. I found her about ten minutes ago and we've been looking for you and waiting for the police and ambulance to come."

The prop man, Jay, came over to stand next to Matthey. "I figure she was maybe trying to get that extension cord that's on top of the work box there. She'd been asking if I had one earlier and I told her I'd get it after dinner. Maybe she tried to jump up and get it and it tangled on the weight and pulled it down on her. Christ, I told her I'd get it for her."

"Did you hear the crash?" Matthey asked.

"Not really, I was in the office and may have heard a dull thud. I had the TV turned up pretty high. That weight should make one loud noise, though."

"Maybe not," the sound man chimed in. "If the weight just hit her head and then kind of just kept hitting her body as she fell, kind of like just rolling onto the floor."

"Yeah, Ronny, that might work," agreed Jay.

"Was anyone else around?" asked Matthey.

"I was the only one downstairs here, apparently," said Jay. Ronny and Charlie were both in the electrics booth.

"Jason was in his dressing room and I was in the office downstairs until I went up to use the bathroom," added Tony. "The rest of the cast haven't come back from dinner, I guess."

Matthey looked at her watch. There were still twenty minutes until the half hour call. "Where's Isabel? I understood she was resting between shows."

"No way she could be here. With all the yelling that was going on those first five minutes she'd have to be deaf not to hear. Everyone here paged you at least twice. We weren't exactly being discreet," said Tony.

The stage doors flew open banging against the walls and Matthey looked around the corner and saw three young serious looking people in white bringing a stretcher up the steps. Edward was in front of them yelling "this way." They quickly made their way to the body and began all the technical methods at their disposal of determining that Carole was, indeed, dead.

"Tony," said Matthey, "please steer all the actors the other way around to their dressing rooms and keep them calm or try to. Assure them everything will be fine and to just concentrate on the show. First, call Norman and see if he wants to try to cancel the Shuberts or at least explain things to them or whatever. Jason, you didn't hear that!"

Jason shrugged. "Most of us figured something was important about tonight. Don't worry, we'll still do a great show."

Matthey sighed. "Yeah, you probably will. Poor Carole. Has anyone notified her family?"

No one nodded.

"O.K., I'll see what I can do. The police should be here any minute. I know they'll want to question everybody so please make sure everything's set onstage and backstage, now, so we don't have to hold the curtain. Ronny, I'll try to get them to talk to you first and you too, Charlie. And me, I guess. And Jason. Well, you don't go onstage for thirty minutes so there is some leeway. Hopefully, I can get them to wait on Tony and Jay until the curtain goes up. I'll be back in two seconds, O.K.?"

Matthey left the paramedics going down their checklist of sure death indications and bounded up the stairs to the dressing rooms. Without knocking she opened the female chorus room. Isabel looked up from the paperback she was reading. Matthey stared for a second, aware that her face was registering several obvious emotions.

"Have you been here since rehearsal ended?"

Isabel smiled at her. If Matthey hadn't been staring into her eyes, she might have found the smile engaging. Instead she exhaled.

"I do not understand. Please say again."

Matthey repeated her question, overly enunciating each word.

"Yes, I do not feel so well so I tell Che it is better if I stay here and rest. Did he not tell you? Did he and you have good dinner?" Her smile grew wider.

Matthey ignored her. Still carefully enunciating she asked, "Didn't you hear all the noise downstairs, over the intercom?" She pointed to the speaker on the wall, seeing Isabel's confused look. "Didn't you understand that Carole was hurt, that there was a big problem? Weren't you at least curious?"

Isabel frowned. "Curious? I do not understand. The, uh," she pointed to the intercom, "was too fast. I could not follow so I give no attention." She waved her hand in a dismissing gesture. "Is something wrong with Carole?" She looked up with a concerned expression.

"Yes, she's dead." The concerned expression remained. "Did you hear a crash or any odd noise?" Since the women's chorus room was right at the top of the stairs, she had the best chance of anyone in the building of hearing something.

Isabel shook her head. "No, just the voices yelling. The performance tonight, they cancel, yes?"

"No. We'll go on, as usual. The police may want to talk to you so stay here, O.K.?"

Isabel nodded and went back to her reading when Matthey didn't add anything further. Matthey closed the door and went back downstairs to find a young and pasty white policeman making notes in his little black book. Someone had found a piece of material, some duvetyn, from the show's reject box and covered Carole. This was fortunate as Tony was already trying to convince a couple of arriving actors that there was nothing worth looking at and to go up to their dressing rooms.

The patrolman, Simpson, told her he was waiting for a police photographer to arrive, along with a forensics expert and a detective. Matthey asked how long he thought the body would remain in the hall. Well, Friday night, he said, lots of action out there, may take awhile for people to free up and make it over here, no telling, really. But not to worry, 'cause, he was sticking around until everything was taken care of. Matthey had visions of everyone stepping over Carole as they crossed from one side of the stage through the hall to the other side. Of course, other than a couple of real quick changes, the cast could go up the stairs to the dressing rooms and then down the stairs on the other side and avoid the backstage area. But still, anyone coming out of the stage right door would see Carole immediately.

Maybe she could set up some kind of flat. She made a mental note to put Tony on that. Just then she saw him coming down the hall from their office.

"I got through to Norman. He said it's too late to head the Shuberts off but he intended to get here by curtain to talk to them. He wanted to know what the hell was going on and why were things getting so chaotic. I told him we were just trying to generate some press."

"Really? I wish you did tell him that. You know he's thinking this would never have happened in the days when he was a Broadway stage manager. And, somehow, I'm to blame for not having been trained in New York. Like I'd be a better stage manager by riding on subways and stepping over phlegm on the sidewalks."

"You did do Rodeo Dr. on Broadway and Chalk It Up to Dust off-Broadway."

"Rodeo bombed and closed fast and Chalk only had a set run of four weeks. When it moved on Broadway, they replaced the director, so I lost out, too. Not very impressive New York credits in Norman's eyes, I fear. Listen, I don't know anything about Carole's family, do you?"

"No, haven't a clue."

"Well, let me try calling around and will you try to talk the cops into letting you put up a flat to block the view, O.K.? And, oh shit, it's half hour. Will you call it? I'll try to help you check the preset."

Matthey went into her office and called Don, the production manager, at his home to see if he knew anything about Carole's background. He didn't and asked if he should come in. She said it couldn't hurt but if he had family obligations he shouldn't worry. Don said he was playing a stimulating game of Pictionary with his six-

129

year-old daughter and that it'd take him about forty minutes to drive down there and that he'd leave as soon as his wife came home.

Matthey called Carole's number and left a message for anyone to call her as soon as possible. The greeting on the machine said 'we' and she thought Carole had talked about a roommate. She put down the receiver and looked up to find Detective Mally standing in the doorway. She sighed. "Apparently, it was an accident," she said.

"Just another coincidence, Ms. Cole?" he said.

O.K., I confess. I killed her and Christine. I'm trying to murder everyone in this company because I'm tired of being indecisive and methodical slaughter seems like a strong statement to make."

"Yes. Do you know what happened?"

Matthey picked up her templet and a pencil and started swirling with her right hand as she gestured Mally to sit somewhere. He picked the couch.

"Actually, I was one of the last to arrive on the scene. My ASM, Tony, found her and then Jay, our prop man showed up. I can tell you who was in the building and, if possible, could you question them in an order that lets us get the show up on time?"

Mally looked amused. "You don't want this to interfere with the performance?"

"The show goes on no matter whose body is lying on the backstage floor. Even mine."

"That's something I'm trying to prevent."

Matthey stopped twirling her templet.

"Where were you before finding Carole?"

Matthey stared at him, thinking, oh shit. "I had gone out to dinner with a friend and he dropped me off outside and the head usher saw me and said something was wrong and I ran in and found her."

"May I ask the name of the friend and what restaurant you were at?"

"Uh, I was with Che Gascon, you know him, and we actually didn't go to a restaurant. I mean, I thought we were, when he asked me to have dinner in order to talk over things, but he drove me to his house and we ate there."

"What did he want to talk over?"

Matthey hoped she didn't look panicked. "Oh, the future of the show, how Isabel was doing, that kind of thing, you know."

"What did you eat?"

"What did we eat?" Matthey forced every cool gene she possessed to the surface. "Uh, we had a glass of wine and he had prepared these hors d'oeuvres things, very good actually."

"That's all?" Mally jotted something down in his book.

"Well, yeah, actually. They were very filling. Lots of cheese and fish and stuff. They filled you up very quickly."

"When did you go to dinner? And I assume Isabel wasn't with you?"

"No, she wasn't feeling well so she stayed in her dressing room to rest. Uh, we left around five o'clock and he dropped me off just a little after seven."

"Two hours for one glass of wine and appetizers."

"And talk. Tonight's an important night for the show. The Shuberts are coming to see it and it may mean we move to Broadway later and my adrenalin is high, and I really wasn't that hungry." Matthey felt more in control now. She heard Tony call fifteen minutes. He stuck his head in the office to say he'd finished onstage and that he'd collect valuables. She smiled gratefully. He also said the police photographer had arrived.

Tony left and Matthey turned back to Detective Mally. "Any more questions?"

"No, not right now. Who should I talk to next?"

"Ronny and Charlie, our sound man and electrician. They were up in the booth and came down when the prop man called them. They shouldn't have much to say. Then talk to Jason, an actor who was upstairs. He doesn't go onstage for the first thirty minutes. Please try not to alarm him, if you can. Then Tony, my assistant, and he'll give you the other names."

Matthey phoned up to Ronny and Charlie. She stood up. She wasn't thrilled with the way Mally was looking at her. She suspected he didn't trust her much anymore. Oh well.

Just as she headed out the door, Tony came running in. "Matthey, Gloria's not here! She's signed in but I've looked everywhere. Her stuff isn't in the dressing room. No one's seen her since she drove off after rehearsal!"

"Page her and call her at home," said Matthey. But she said it without conviction. The sinking feeling swept over again as once again she headed toward Isabel's dressing room.

Chapter Twenty-One

Matthey ran into Bonita, the wardrobe mistress, as she headed upstairs. Quickly, she told her to expect that Isabel would be onstage instead of Gloria. Costumes weren't really a problem. The one real outfit that 'Danais' wears should fit. But it was in four pieces and since it was put on as a quick change it would be wise for Bonita and Isabel to try it on and talk through the forty-five second change. She yelled back to Tony to see if he could find Norman.

She ran up the stairs and threw open the women's chorus room door. Three faces looked up. Two belonged to Kiley and Laura, the other female understudies and the third, strikingly beautiful face belonged to Isabel. Christ, Matthey thought, she looks exquisite.

"You've put on make-up! You look incredible."

"Thank you," replied Isabel. "I was just trying things."

"Well, it's perfect. Isabel, we don't know where Gloria is so unless she arrives in the next ten minutes, you're on. How comfortable do you feel about that?"

"I am quite confident. I know my words and the, uh, blocking."

"I hope so. How about the nudity? Will that bother you?"

"I am quite fine with that. It is not a problem."

Matthey sighed. "I sure hope so. O.K., Bonita will be up in a second to try on the house dress. When you hear Tony call places, go to stage right." She pointed to the SR side. "He'll always be in the wings and will be there for your exits and entrances. Just pay attention to the other actors and trust them if they steer you, direct you one way or the other. One thing that concerns me are the blackouts. How are you at seeing in the dark?"

"It is no problem. I have very good eyes."

"Yes, of course you do." Matthey stifled a nervous giggle. There was only one blackout she had to worry about, anyway. She made a mental note to hold it an extra couple of seconds.

"One more thing. The few times you do speak you must make sure you're loud enough. Don't shout--just pretend you're in a conversation with someone sitting in the last row. Don't yell at them, just make sure they can hear you, O.K.? Listen to the level that the other actors are speaking at and try to match them."

"Yes, it will be no problem."

"Right. If you're nervous, don't worry. Everyone is. Just try to turn it into energy. You're beautiful and bright and you'll be wonderful."

"Thank you."

"Do you have any more information about Carole?" asked Kiley, a forty-two-year old, aerobicized redhead who has signed ninety per cent of her professional contracts as an understudy. She was just on the cusp of either becoming an embittered actor or acknowledging her probable continued singlehood and

134

undistinguished success and embracing a healthy maternal concern
for those around her. So far, Kiley's positive days still far
outnumbered her occasional depressive times when she wore the same
clothes for days and was usually seen asleep.

"No, not really. Uh, I imagine they'll be taking her away fairly
soon. We've put a flat up. The police will be here for awhile asking
questions. Oh shit, they'll want to talk to you, Isabel. Well, hell by
the time Tony tells Mally your name you'll be onstage so we'll deal
with that later. Call if you need something. Tony will meet you stage
right." Usually, Matthey hugged an understudy who was about to go
on, but Isabel's demeanor caused her to hesitate.

"Uh, good luck, O.K." Matthey chose not to say "break a leg"
assuming Isabel had never heard of it.

"Yes, thank you."

As Matthey turned to leave, Bonita burst through the door
with the dress. She nodded at her and, leaving them, headed for the
other dressing rooms. As quickly as possible, she informed the other
actors about Isabel, asked them to take care of her, assured them all
would be fine and avoided any lengthy questioning. She ran
downstairs to check with Tony. As she headed toward the office the
looming figure of Dr. Tom suddenly rose in front of her.

"Matthey, there you are. You've had sex, haven't you. You
look flushed."

"Dr. Tom, would you please shut up. We're having some
problems here and I've been running around. Why are you here,
anyway?"

"Why to see you, of course. I picked up the tickets you got for
me and I thought it would be fun to run around backstage and say hi
and maybe get a glimpse of all that exciting preshow theatre stuff."

"Uh, Dr. Tom, I forgot you were coming tonight. Uh, listen, now isn't a great time to talk, but, maybe after the show you could come backstage and I'll show you around. Where's your date?"

"She kept me waiting in her living room for fifteen minutes and I decided I would assert myself in the relationship. I figured I should start on the first date. So, when she went to find her purse, I left. When I call her in a couple of days I expect to talk to a very contrite woman."

"Only if she answers the phone. Did you turn in the other ticket to the box office?"

"No, there was this wonderfully assertive older gentleman that had the most amazing collection of beer cans in his shopping cart. He said he'd probably get ten dollars from just beer cans, empty beer cans, not even cleaned. Amazing. You know, he was once a train engineer. A real one, with the cap and overalls, the whole outfit. Even blew the whistle. He's wonderful. He was out in the plaza trying to get a little extra money by singing Frankie Laine songs. And you know how much I love Frankie Laine."

"No kidding! You love Frankie Laine? Like hell you do. I love Frankie Laine."

"There you are. I told him I couldn't give him any money, but he was welcome to the ticket. He took it and said he'd come in when he figured out where to stash his beer cans. What's behind that flat over there and why are policemen here?"

"Oh, those are just actors and the flat needs painting. Listen, I have to go. Enjoy the show. Clap loudly. I'll see you later."

"Bye. I know, you know."

"Huh? Nevermind. Bye. Which song was he singing?"

"Who?"

"The beer can guy."

"Oh, 'Jezebel' and 'Moonlight Gambler'."

Matthey looked pained. "No kidding. I love those!" Dr. Tom went out the back door and Matthey continued on to the office. Ronny and Charlie were shaking hands with Detective Mally.

"Hi, are you all finished?"

"Yeah, we're heading upstairs now. Talk to you in a few minutes."

She turned to Mally. Over the speaker she heard Tony call five minutes. "When do you think you'll remove Carole?"

"Probably shortly after the show starts. You say Jason is the next one to talk to?"

"Yes. I'll page him to come down."

"Have you found your actress, Gloria?"

"No. I've made plans for the understudy to go on. I'm sure Gloria is fine and there's a perfectly good explanation. I just hope she hasn't been in an accident."

"Like Christine?"

"That wasn't what I meant. Look, as you can obviously tell, things are a bit chaotic around here. Right now, I'm concerned about a young girl going onstage in a pivotal role with no rehearsal.

"I might be more concerned about the large number of people on this show who are dead or missing."

"Being concerned about that right this minute won't make the show better."

"The show must go on."

"Yes, it do." Matthey tugged on her hair. "Look, can you put someone on finding Gloria? Of course, I'm worried. I had heard earlier that she wanted to talk to me, and I planned to do that tonight."

"Isabel must be awfully excited. This is a big break for her, isn't it?"

"Yes, it could be if she were prepared and rehearsed. I just hope we get through it."

"Does her friend, Che, know?"

"I have no idea. I didn't tell him. But he told me he'd be here so I'm sure he is."

Tony came into the office. "Any word on Gloria?"

"No, none. Isabel's ready, Bonita's up there with her now. I told her you'd be in the wings. What about you?"

"No answer on the cell. Just the machine. I told Norman and split quickly before he could start yelling. I'm surprised he's not back here, but I think a Shubert guy was with him. Did you talk to the other actors?"

"Yeah. They were fine, pretty much. I guess after hearing about Carole, not much more can surprise them. I wish I'd talked to Gloria before dinner. She give you any indication what was bothering her?"

"Not really. Just got the feeling it was important, and she wanted to talk before the performance."

"O.K. Try to keep up people's morale back here and watch Isabel. She seems awfully secure, though. Maybe she'll be fine. Thank God there's not much dialogue."

"I looked for Alan but you know he never shows up until just before curtain. I told Norman that Alan didn't know and to tell him if he sees him."

"Good. I feel terrible that there's no one to call about Carole."

"Terrible enough to cancel the show?" asked Detective Mally.

"No. I know you don't understand," said Matthey.

"I could shut it down for you, but I'm interested in it going on, I think. I'll be back here all night."

138

"Sure. Help yourself. O.K., Tony, might as well call places. I'm going up. Hope for the best. Talk to you on headset." She gathered up her script, notebook and stopwatch.

"Oh, Matthey. I forgot. Roger called you earlier. Said you had to call. Very important."

"Well, it will have to wait. If he calls again tell him I'll try to get him after the show. Oh, and page Jason for Detective Mally, please."

Matthey edged her way past Mally. She looked at him briefly and didn't like the intense look he gave her in return. She headed around the corner, heard Bonita yell out that everything was fine, grabbed a cup of coffee and walked upstairs.

Very gingerly she climbed the steep ladder that led to the grid and the booth. Walking across the catwalk she was careful not to spill any coffee on the heads of the audience below her. It was strictly forbidden to have liquids in the grid. She loved the risk. Others took up sky diving. Matthey preferred taking the chance of pouring hot liquid on the heads of the paying public thereby risking law suits, and career disgrace.

She opened the door to her cubicle, put the script on the table, slid into her chair and picked up her handset. She pushed in the button.

"Hi, guys. Well, this should be a good one!"

Chapter Twenty-Two

Matthey continued, "Ronny, I'm going to have to make an announcement. Gloria's not here and the understudy's going on."

Ronny's voice came over the biscuit next to her. "You've got to be kidding! Is she sick?"

"No, just missing. Hope she's not dead, too."

"God, you think so?" Charlie's voice piped in.

"Well, it seems to be going around." Matthey took out her performance report and filled in the date, day and performance number. Looking through her window at the seated crowd below she filled in an approximate percentage of the capacity of the house. Tony's voice came over the speaker.

"Hi, we're in place. So far, everyone alive five minutes ago is still alive and here."

"Thanks, Tony. How's Isabel?"

"Calm and collected. She's sitting in the wing with Gloria's bathrobe on. Che showed up and ushered her into Gloria's dressing room. It was easier to let it go."

"Yeah, of course." Wonder what Che thought about all this. Ecstatic, probably. "Thanks, Tony, take care of her and good luck."

"You, too. I'll keep you posted on events backstage."

Tony turned off his headset and Matthey began her series of warnings and cue lights. As the house lights dimmed to half she watched Norman kiss three more cheeks of well dressed women and say a final word to the men she assumed must be the infamous Shuberts. None of them carried the name of Shubert, of course, but they represented the Shubert money and power and that was enough to set everyone in the production on edge. Other producers were capable of moving the show to Broadway but somehow only the 'Shuberts' conjured up images of 1940s movies showing serious-looking, silent bald men lurking in the back rows of the darkened rows of theatre houses playing God with artistic futures.

Matthey made the announcement letting the audience know that an understudy would be going on. She then took the house and preset to black, cued the sound and, at the appropriate point in the music, brought the stage lights up revealing the sun rising on the South American plantation. 'Jacques' was standing by the fence looking at the offstage corral. In his hand he held a .38 revolver. As the music swelled to the specified arpeggio 'Jacques' raised the gun, aimed it offstage and fired. Matthey cued the soundtrack of the horse whinnying and as 'Jacques' fired again Matthey called the sound to bump out and there was instant silence. The audience gasped.

Alright, great, Matthey thought. Whenever they reacted strongly to the shooting, they proved to be a responsive group throughout. In five minutes, Isabel would make her entrance as 'Danais'.

Matthey wrote the time the show started on the report and penciled in information under the 'Absent' and 'Replacement' columns. She'd have a lot to say in the 'Notes' section. At this point there was no point in worrying. Isabel would either be wonderful, terrible or something in-between. All she could do is try to cover her cue-wise if the actress messed up. But the whole game was now in Isabel's ballpark. It was up to her and the rest of the cast. Everyone else was support.

Matthey watched and listened as the actors set up the necessary exposition. They were hot tonight. A heightened adrenalin. Obviously, a combination of knowing the Shuberts were in the house, dealing with the deaths, and a new understudy onstage. It was amazing they weren't keeling over from nervous breakdowns with all the stress they were under. The resilience of actors always amazed her. When they were onstage. Offstage, the complaints and whining made a hyperactive two-year old seem like a saint. But once the curtain rose the majority of actors persevered and rose above anything getting in the way of their performance, be it injury, illness, personal tragedy, hatred of another performer or knowing an inexperienced understudy would need their help every step of the way. After the show, however, they'd complain bitterly about every bit of it. Tolerance of understudies onstage was bountiful. Intolerance of them offstage knew no end.

'Jacques', left alone onstage once again, dropped to his knees and started digging in the dirt. He seemed to be looking for something. As he glanced up with the rehearsed expression on his face that signaled the possibility of him having found something, Matthey cued the light that brightened the upright area of the stage. Isabel walked into the area and stood there.

The second gasp of the evening was heard. She was beautiful! There wasn't a hint of self-consciousness about standing in front of over seven hundred people with nothing more on her body than a necklace. When Matthey cued the music that represented the record player in the house playing, 'Danais' began to dance in a manner that made every man in the audience place his program over his lap and every woman want to put their arms around her and make her some hot soup.

Gloria had a lovely body, a southern California aerobic physique. Trim and hard. Isabel's was soft and lush. Slim but a body that would yield to a touch not cause a bruise. Gloria's body, like millions of others, was craft. Isabel's was an art.

'Jacques' stood up and turned around to see 'Danais' for the first time. Matthey could see that the actor, Jackson Cass, was visibly shaken. He recovered quickly and went through the directed blocking of crossing upstage to greet her, discover her inability to speak the language and lead her down stage to discover where she came from. Jackson carried the major burden of this scene as 'Danais' simply reacted to the plantation owner's questions. However, Isabel was simply exquisite. Her combination of innocence and inherent sexuality were breathtaking. Even when 'Jacques' put his horse blanket over her as he seated her, Matthey knew that all eyes in the audience remained on Isabel.

"She's wonderful, isn't she?" Matthey spun around.

"Damn it, Che. I told you not to come up here."

Che came up behind her and shifted her chair back so that she once again faced the stage. He put his hands on her neck and started rubbing the back of her head with his thumbs. "I wouldn't want you to miss any cues. As you can see, your fears about any self-consciousness were unfounded."

"She is beautiful but these first couple of scenes don't really require any real acting. What's she going to be like in the picnic scene or when she first meets 'Louis'?"

"She will be wonderful. You worry too much. We have worked very hard on her acting."

"Che, I don't understand why you're up here. Wouldn't you rather be in the audience where you can feel the audience response? It's a lot more fun in the house."

Che's right hand slipped inside Matthey's shirt and covered her breast. Matthey immediately removed it. "No, right now I have to concentrate on the show. Please. I have enough on my mind as it is."

"Yes, of course. The Shuberts are very important."

"Che, how did you know about them?"

"Oh, I heard it mentioned, I don't know, someone backstage, perhaps. Why didn't you tell me at dinner?" He grabbed her hand and pulled it behind her, pressing it upon him. He was rock hard. Again, she pulled away, beginning to get annoyed.

"I mean it, stop it. This is work. I think you should go downstairs. Now!" Matthey called three more cues.

"The Shuberts will love Isabel." His hands rested lightly on her shoulders. "They will insist she be in the show."

"I think you're being a little naive. The Shuberts are just interested in whether the show will make money. The play would probably be recast anyway."

"I think you are the one who is naive. The Shuberts are men. Yes, they'll recast, put stars in the leads, but, to discover an incredible, new, exceptionally talented, gorgeous young woman would also be good box office. Besides, there are others, who are also important in the audience.

How the hell did he know that, Matthey thought. She didn't know that.

Just then the third gasp of the evening was heard. 'Danais' had stood up quickly knocking the horse blanket to the ground and was turned upstage facing away from 'Jacques' and the audience. Starting on the back of her right shoulder and crossing down over her left buttocks was a twisting, gnarly scar that resembled a giant seguro cactus.

"My God, Che, what's that?"

"Oh, Isabel had an unfortunate accident when she was a child. It should fade with time. It already has. I think it's quite striking."

"Striking! Why didn't you tell us? Half the audience will think it's real and lose their concentration and the other half will think it's intentional and wait for it to be brought up in the script. Jesus, what kind of accident did that?"

"Again, you worry too much. It will make them sympathetic to her and they will soon forget it."

"Jackson must be pissed. He knows he'll look very callous when he doesn't say anything about it. He also knows it's upstaging the hell out of him."

Just then 'Jacques' stood up. While still saying the lines about how he would let her have the room over the kitchen he picked up the horse blanket and walked up behind her. He hesitated for an instant and then lightly ran a finger over the scar near her neck. His expression registered a horror for a fraction of a second and then he slipped the blanket over her, turned her around and offered her his arm to lead her off stage.

That's great, Matthey thought. What a pro. I love him, perfect way to handle it.

'Danais' flashed 'Jacques' a huge smile and the audience burst into applause as they walked off and the next scene began. As Matthey called the cues, she couldn't help but admire Isabel's handling of the incident, as well. Maybe Che was right. Christ, that must have been some accident. Poor girl.

Tony's voice came over the biscuit. "Matthey, Gloria just showed up. She's a mess. Seems she was mugged. I don't know the

145

details, but she wants to know if she can go on in the next scene and assume the role."

Oh shit.

"Tony, tell her I'm very sorry, I wish she could, but it would be unnecessarily confusing at this point. If Isabel were awful, maybe, but she's doing well, and I can't justify putting Gloria on. Tell her we love her and to talk to Mally who, I assume, is still there and to go home if she wants to. Or not. Try to make her feel better, O.K. You know what to say."

Tony assured her he would do all he could.

Matthey put down the handset. "You know, Che, you better expect the police to question you two pretty closely. Ignoring Carole's death--"

"Which all of you seem to be doing rather well," interjected Che.

"Yeah, well, as I was saying, except for that, one could make a case that the one person benefitting from Christine's death and Gloria's mugging is Isabel. And, I suppose, you."

Che's hands started massaging her neck. "Oh, Matthey. You make love to me, but you do not trust me. That is so American. So cynical. I'm disappointed in you. You think Isabel's scar is ugly. I think it's beautiful and unique. You think you can't work because my hand is caressing your breast. I think you'll simply enjoy the work more. You waste too much time, worry too much. Embrace each moment. Life can end so quickly."

He reached down and began to kiss her neck. As she protested, he gripped her wrists and held them to her sides. He reached down with his mouth and suckled her left breast, moistening her blouse.

Matthey began to panic. "Che, I have to call a cue. The scene's ending. 'Danais' is coming back onstage."

Che released her right wrist and Matthey grabbed the handset. "Hi, you guys," she said as casually as possible. "Che decided to pay me a visit in the booth. Warning on Lights 8 through 10.5 and Sound D and D1."

"What the hell is he doing up there?" Charlie barked. "Tell him to get the hell out and be quiet doing it."

Matthey called her cues and watched Isabel walk back onstage now dressed in an overly large cook's apron. She turned around to face Che, halfway expecting to find him gone. He was standing at the door with a sad smile on his face.

"Ola, Matthey. I am sorry. I hope you discover what you want. You will always bring a smile to my heart." Che disappeared through the door.

Matthey sighed. It is all too much, I think. I really do. She turned back to the show.

Chapter Twenty-Three

'Danais' stood stage right on the second-floor balcony and waved down to 'Louis', the nephew. Her innocence and enthusiasm radiated from her as if she was backlit by Pollyanna's personal sunbeam. Actually, it was a leko with an amber gel. Annie was a good lighting designer.

'Louis' waved to her and then turned his back on 'Danais' to face downstage and the audience. With one hand he took the Ten of Spades from his shirt pocket and removed the cigarette from his mouth with the other and used the lit end to ignite the playing card. As it burned and 'Danais' beamed, Matthey called the final fade of the act. The house lights came up and the audience filed out for the intermission fairly confident that this rain forest burning and likely drug dealing nephew would cause 'Danais' to lose her smile in the second act. Matthey was pleased that the applause didn't stop until the house lights were at full.

She entered the time that the act ended on her report, reset her stopwatch to start the intermission and noted that the house dress would need re-hemming if Isabel went on for any length of time.

"But, of course, that won't be likely," Matthey mumbled to herself. "Right."

She grabbed her empty coffee cup and tossed it in the trashcan as she exited to the grid. Running down the steps she hurried backstage. As she turned into the stage manager office, she found

Gloria and Detective Mally sitting on her couch. She could see that Gloria had been crying.

"Oh, my God, Gloria, I'm so sorry. Are you alright? Were you hurt?" She hugged the actor and felt guilty that so many conflicting thoughts were crossing her mind.

"Tony said you wouldn't let me go on. The Shuberts are out there and I should be doing the second act. You could make an announcement. Please, you know how important this is. For the show's sake. She hasn't even rehearsed." Gloria looked as miserable as one could possibly look. She sat down again, huddling into Mally.

The detective looked at Matthey with a "well, so now what are you going to do" look on his face. He even put his arm around Gloria's shoulder. Prick, Matthey thought.

"Gloria, I know it's unfair. If Isabel were really bad, I could justify it but she's doing well enough. Not as good as you would, of course, that would be impossible, but to the audience she's acceptable. They don't know the difference and I have to consider the overall show. Changing actors in the middle of the show, unless it's absolutely necessary, is unfair to the audience and unfair to the show. I know Norman and Alan will tell the Shuberts that you're much better. They're just looking at the play not the actors. If they're serious about the show they'll be back to see it again. And if by some miracle this show should move, the producers are going to pay a great deal of credence to what Alan wants. The director has a lot of power in these things. A producer might insist upon a star or refuse to use someone they consider terrible but otherwise Alan has the major control in the casting. Really. And he loves you, you know that." Matthey hoped she sounded as sincere as she was trying to look.

149

"Matthey, I know this sounds terrible but she's not as good, is she? Oh God, I'm sorry, I don't want to be one of those kind of people."

"Don't be silly. Of course, you're better. The rest of the cast is being wonderful and helping her out tremendously. They're being very professional and I'm really proud of them. But you know they're under a lot of stress that wouldn't be there if you were in the role." Or if they didn't have to step over Carole on their way to places. "I know this is hard but tomorrow you'll be back up there and there are still other producers coming, not to mention the critics and opening night."

"Other producers?"

"Sure, the Shuberts aren't the only game in town."

"If it's alright with you, I'd like to go home now. Please tell Isabel she was terrific and that I just couldn't stay, O.K.?"

"I think you're smart to go on home. I'll give the whole cast your love. And I know they'll be very happy to have you back onstage tomorrow. Are you alright to drive?"

"Yes, Detective Mally has been wonderful. One of his men is going to drive me to my car and then follow me home. Thanks, Matthey. I'll see you at one o'clock tomorrow."

"Yeah, take care, O.K.? Soak in a hot bath and try to sleep. It'll all work out fine." She hugged Gloria again and watched her leave the room. Then she turned back to the officer.

"So, what happened to her anyway?"

"Should I consider that a satisfactory handling of the situation?" He was giving her the 'I'm still going to be a prick' look.

"Look, I don't know whether it was successful or not. I like Gloria. This is a lousy situation. I hope it works out for her."

"Isabel is really doing well, isn't she?"

"She's doing great. The audience loves her. And I am willing to bet there's a good chance that Norman will push Alan to keep her. Gloria's very good but Isabel has a quality that's hard to match."

"And the rest of the cast?"

"They'll be upset but they'd be more upset if they were getting fired and since they're not, they'll adjust. And basically, on some level, they know Isabel's better. The main hurdle is that everyone adores Gloria and Isabel has not exactly endeared herself to the company."

"Because of her lack of English?"

"No, that's not it. She comes across as a bloody cold person."

"She doesn't on that little monitor you've got up there." He pointed toward the television set up in the corner.

"Yeah, well, I guess that means she can act. Poor Gloria, she must hate Christine right now for dying."

"Gloria said she stopped at a convenience store on her way back to the theatre. She had dinner with a friend and was stopping to pick up some toothpaste. It was a corner Mom and Pop store with a parking lot behind off an alley. As she returned to her car a guy popped up from behind the truck parked next to her. He punched her in the face, grabbed her purse and threw it in the back of the pick-up. Another guy appeared and they pulled her into the front seat of the truck and took off."

"Oh, my God, she was raped!" Matthey finally sat down. She wanted to cry.

"No, she wasn't. They kept yelling at her in Spanish, I think assuming she'd understand them. Apparently, Gloria doesn't speak Spanish. It's interesting, neither do her parents. She's third generation. Guess we just assume things. Anyway, after driving around for about twenty minutes they pushed her out of the pick-up.

151

They had driven up into Griffith Park and she was let out near the top. The park was closed so no one was around. Walking down, she accepted a ride from a young couple in a convertible and persuaded them to drive her straight here. She thought she might have been able to get here in time if you held the curtain."

"If she'd called, I would have held the curtain."

"I guess she forgot that the show always goes on." Mally smiled at her. "I've taken down all the information and, hopefully, we'll get lucky. She found her purse on the side of the road halfway down. The money was gone but everything else was there."

"Doesn't that sound like kind of a strange crime? Why drive her around? Why not just take her purse in the beginning. They evidently didn't intend to hurt her. Seems weird.

"Almost as if they just wanted to make sure she didn't get to the theatre in time to go on."

Since Matthey had already reached that conclusion near the beginning of the story, she had her response formulated.

"Che was with me until ten after seven. And he was back in the theatre around ten of eight. And Isabel was in the theatre the whole time. Granted Che was gone during the crucial time but there's no way he could know where Gloria was going for dinner and that she would stop at that particular store at that time. Besides Gloria knows Che."

"Has Che mentioned any friends? Any names at all? Any messages left for either of them?"

"You can ask Lou, the doorman. He'd be the one taking them. But no, I haven't heard anyone mentioned."

The phone rang. Matthey expected to hear a voice asking for Che. She answered it quickly. It was Roger. "Hi, look, this isn't a good time to call. Things are really crazy down here. Yeah, the

Shuberts and other things. Yeah, I heard you were looking for me. O.K., sure, we can talk after. I'll call. Uh, O.K., I'll meet you after. It might be late. O.K., I'll see you, then. Yeah, meet me there. Just be prepared to wait. O.K. Bye." She hung up and looked at Mally.

Tony ran in and looked surprised to see her sitting there. "Wow, you look relaxed. Thought you'd be tensed up just for empathy, if nothing else."

"Trust me, I am. You just caught me between adrenalin rushes. Detective Mally's been telling me about Gloria. How's the cast holding up. Isabel's doing well." Matthey sighed.

"The cast is fine. They know she's good. No one wants to say it, though. But everyone's very up. When are they taking Carole out of here?"

"Oh, Christ." Matthey looked horrified. "You mean she's still laying over there."

Mally stood up. "Yes, Friday night is very active, unfortunately. Hopefully soon. Meanwhile, I'm going up to Isabel's dressing room and see if I can find Che. I didn't see him anywhere during the first act. I've already informed Isabel I expect to talk to her after the show."

"I saw Che up in the booth during the first act. I don't expect him up there again, however."

As Mally gazed on her, Matthey felt naked. Not physically, but mentally. She felt like her thoughts and actions for the past five days were up on a billboard on Sunset strip with big footlights illuminating every ambivalent moment.

Mally didn't say anything as he passed her and headed upstairs. "Oh, she's in Gloria's dressing room, number four," she called out to his back.

She turned back to Tony. "Guess he already knows that." Tony had a very disagreeable smirk on his face. He also remained nonverbal and ran out the door to call "five".

"Shit." Matthey picked up the phone and dialed Bill's number. The machine answered and beeped. "Hi, Bill, I'm going to be home really late tonight. I'm probably having a nervous breakdown but I don't have time to check. This just seems to be one of those days when just a heck of a lot is going on. You name it, it's happening here. Gosh, I thought you'd be home. Oh, well, see you when I get there. I might wake you up. It's a crazy time. Bye." She hung up and sighed again.

Alan stuck his head in as he passed by. "Norman loves her. Lonny, the Shubert guy wants to meet her and the talk in the lobby is great. We need to talk after the show. Anyone hear from Gloria?"

"Yeah, she showed up just after curtain. She was mugged. She talked to the police here and went home when she realized she couldn't go on."

"Shit, that's bad. Poor kid. Gather the company right after the show. I'll just take a few minutes. Then you and I talk. The show is just great, huh." He ran on, heading back to the front of house with a big grin on his face.

Yeah, poor kid, Matthey thought. She made a mental note to tell the house manager to make sure there were real house boards for the understudies tomorrow. No more scribbled signs. God, she felt like a hypocrite. Other people must handle these things better. Or maybe handling them worse was what she should be doing. Hell, the show must go on. But not only that, the best show must go on. Face it, Matthey, even if you discover that Che and Isabel were responsible for Christine and Gloria, and all of Syria and North Korea, there's still that part of you that knows you'd still want Isabel in the role simply

154

because she's very, very good. Art stands alone. Purity and impurity can both result in art. What counts is the art. You don't fuck with that. Oh, shit. Debbie and Ben. Definitely time to call them. Ben might want to see her before she goes to jail, I suppose. Or help her choose an agent. I wonder what's going on in Isabel's mind. And Che's.

Matthey looked at herself in the mirror. Tussling her hair, she sighed and ran upstairs to say hello to the actors before going up for the second act.

Chapter Twenty-Four

She stopped on the top step upon hearing the sweet, fingernail-on-chalkboard, dulcet tones of a female voice screaming "If you stop me, I'll kill you." Matthey raced around the corner to dressing room #4, now occupied by Isabel. She froze in the doorway staring in the wall mirror at the reflected image of Detective Mally's gutted belly. His green checked shirt now had a rather riveting display of red streaking downward from a horizontal slash. A button was hanging from a single thread. He was standing slumped over clutching at his stomach.

On the floor at the policeman's feet lay the crumpled and awfully lifeless appearing body of Che. He appeared to have a head wound. In the far corner, Isabel was backed against the wall looking as pale as an albino polar bear who's seen a ghost. She seemed to be trying to become intimate with the molding.

To her left, in front of the make-up table stood Gloria, holding the prop knife that "Jacques" used to carve his table sculptures. It was a six-inch long blade. Usually, prop knives are dulled to avoid injury but the scene called for the character to actually whittle a wooden python onstage.

Matthey wondered if the police would have to confiscate it, and how they'd be able to replace it for the second act. Then she realized there probably wouldn't be one. Instinctively, she grabbed the gun from the policeman's shoulder holster, visible as he bent over. She held it on Gloria. With her other hand she gestured the gathering group of actors to stay back and not to move.

"O.K., Gloria, relax now, it's going to be alright. Everything will be fine. Put the knife down very slowly on the table, O.K. We're going to straighten all of this out."

Gloria stared at her from eyes that reflected the chaos of her mind. She didn't move. Neither did anyone else. Mally was still holding his guts in but his eyes were on Gloria and he looked alert.

"I know how upsetting all of this has been for you, Gloria. Everyone here knows you're the best one in this role. Tony told me that even Isabel told him she couldn't wait until the night was over and you were back in the role. She's petrified out there. You're the only one who can do it. But we can't let anything more happen in this room because we want you to be free to go on tomorrow, O.K.?"

Gloria emitted a low, hissing, guttural burst. "I want to go on now."

"Well, let me ask Isabel. Do you mind if Gloria goes on for the second act?"

All eyes went to the statue in the corner. Very slowly, her head shook and a barely audible "no" came out.

"There, you see, it's fine, you can do the second act. Just put the knife down and let's get you cleaned up, O.K.?"

Gloria backed away slowly and put the knife on the table. Matthey lowered the gun to her side and walked around Mally. "O.K., Gloria, that's great."

She called back to the other actors standing in the hall. "Guys, we're going to have a new 'Danais' again. I know you'll all be relieved to have Gloria back. We have to hurry. Make sure you all are ready. We'll do another announce before curtain."

Matthey turned back to Gloria. "Now, we'll have to do something quickly about your hair. Oh, Isabel, would you take the bracelets off so we can get them on Gloria."

157

As Isabel slowly took off the jewelry, Matthey kept talking and worked her way up to just in front of Gloria. Gloria's right hand was still within inches from the knife.

"That's great, Isabel, just hand them here and I'll help Gloria. I'm so glad this is all working out. Here, give me your hand and I'll get this on. You know, Alan and the audience will be thrilled to know the real 'Danais' is back. Luckily, you won't need too much make-up. We need to be quick about this."

As the young actor held out her right hand, Matthey quickly grabbed the knife and flipped it behind her. She heard a gasp from Isabel and looked back. The knife had stuck in the back of Che's thigh. Che didn't seem bothered by it.

However, Gloria lunged at Matthey who immediately tossed the gun aside. It discharged as it hit the floor but no one yelled so she guessed all was fine. Within seconds, Detective Mally had jumped forward and secured Gloria. Together, they managed to handcuff her. She lay on the floor in a sullen, crumpled heap next to Che. Matthey looked at him and realized the gun had discharged into Che's side. God, she thought, I hope he was dead before.

Just then Mally collapsed on top of both Gloria and Che and it occurred to Matthey that it might be time to yell for the policeman downstairs, and to get an ambulance. Where the hell was Tony? Didn't anyone hear the shot? Someone needs to be dealing with the audience who was, undoubtedly, filing in for the second act. Just then she heard the loudspeaker burst out with "Places, please, places for the second act."

Christ, should I? Mally's out and the cop downstairs is a twenty-year old idiot. Why not, eh?

Quickly, she told Isabel to get downstairs into places, everything would be fine. Hurrying into the hall, she assured the actors that they should get into places and do the best they can. She knew the actors on the men's side of the dressing room area hadn't heard anything and would be assembling anyway. The women in the cast went running downstairs. She had to admit, it surprised her that they acquiesced so easily.

She ran downstairs as well, told Lou, the doorman, to call an ambulance immediately. She found Tony in the wings and filled him in quickly. Said once the show was up, to make sure the ambulance came in the back door and not through the house. She then went over to the policeman and said that Detective Mally was upstairs in the dressing room and had been stabbed and that the suspect was handcuffed and that an ambulance was on the way. She said she'd be right up. The young cop looked like he was the one who'd been stabbed and raced upstairs.

She then went into her office and phoned the light booth and instructed Charlie to go ahead and start the show. There were no sound cues at the top so all he had to do was take the house lights out and bring up the stage lights. He was confused and hesitant but agreed. She watched the monitor and called the cues while watching the screen. She relaxed when she saw the lights come up and all the actors were in the correct places. She ran upstairs to join the young policeman.

Quickly, she filled him in as much as she could. It was only then that she realized she didn't know much. Gloria hadn't moved. Detective Mally was still out but breathing well. The policeman confirmed that Che was dead. He'd already placed a call to the police ,and she knew they'd be here momentarily. She excused herself and found Tony. He said he'd talked to the front of house and that there were two ushers outside waiting to direct all police and ambulances to the stage door. She asked him to go up to the booth and call the show

159

as best he could. He knew her style of writing cues and he knew the show and she figured it would work out well enough. There was no way she could justify going up there herself. Tony said sure, and she went to alert Lou that all hell would shortly break loose back here and to just try to keep them confined to backstage and not to let them go into the wings or in the house. He looked at her like she was crazy. She figured she probably was. Boy, do I want a drink.

She waited with the young policeman.

"Chuck Lynch is my name. Officer Lynch."

It didn't seem to bother him that the show was continuing. Of course, it might have helped that she'd turned down the monitor in the room so he couldn't actually hear the show. Gloria was sitting there, just rocking back and forth. Actually, that was what, at first ,prompted her to turn off the show volume. It agitated Gloria too much, hearing the other actors.

Christ, Matthey thought, why the hell did she kill Che, instead of Isabel. Mally must have been awfully surprised when that sweet little thing he was cuddling so protectively downstairs turned around and tried to do a little liposuction on his belly. Hell, I'm surprised. Gloria was one of the nicest people I ever met. I must be losing my touch. What good is a stage manager who's a lousy judge of character.

Oh, can it, you knew Che was of questionable character and you still slept with him.

But that's the difference, I knew it beforehand. I wasn't taken in. Therefore, it's not the same thing.

Ah.

She was sitting in the room holding Detective Mally's hand when she heard the roar downstairs of feet stampeding and excited voices. They headed up in her direction.

160

Within minutes Mally was loaded on a gurney and hauled off to the waiting ambulance. A police photographer took a million pictures and then a couple of minutes later Che was taken off in the same direction but to a difference ambulance, and Gloria was undergoing questioning by two very large detectives. Another detective looking about the age of fifty-five, with thinning black hair, was drilling Matthey.

"I really haven't much to tell. I came into the room after everything happened. All I can do is speculate on what I've told you."

"Where is this Isabel? Mexican, huh. Got a green card? Get her in here for questioning immediately."

She hated him. "Uh, she's onstage right now. She'll be done in a half an hour. The other actors, as well. I know they'll want to help you as much as possible. Uh, Detective Mally felt it was important that the show continue as he felt, I think, it might be enlightening to the recent events. So, of course, I didn't want to interfere with that and insisted they do the second act. Gosh, I hope that's alright? I probably wasn't thinking too clearly." Matthey was nauseating herself. But it seemed to be working.

The balding detective gave Chuck Lynch such a withering look the young cop appeared ready to cry. He disappeared from the room.

Sorry, Matthey thought.

"Miss Cole, I think continuing a performance of this show was a very stupid choice and I'm furious that you were allowed to do so. However, at this point I'll let it continue. Mally may have had reasons we don't know about. You better hope so. I'm stationing officers in the house as well as back here. Now get this woman down to headquarters immediately." He gestured to Gloria.

161

As the still silent Gloria was led out, Matthey found herself once again relating the feeble details of her story. It took only a few minutes. As they sat in the blood-soaked dressing room she heard actors quietly come upstairs to make costume changes and just as quietly go back down. No one poked their head in to ask questions. She supposed they realized the importance of keeping a low profile, in order to have the show continue. Or maybe they were just staying in character. With actors, anything's possible. She wondered if the male performers had been clued in yet. Even if they knew, hell, what's a few more bodies.

The policemen took pictures and dusted and wrote in their notebooks. Where were they for Carole? She's probably still lying down there. I bet they didn't even take her away in an ambulance.

"Sir," Matthey started, "you know, we've been waiting for three hours for someone to take away the body we have downstairs. I just thought I'd point that out to you, in case, you were unaware."

The arm of the law glared at her. "Don't get cute with me."

Uh, O.K. "Can I turn up the volume there so I can hear the show?"

Again, the glare but the policeman stepped over and turned it up himself.

The final scene was in progress. The voices didn't sound comfortable and their rhythms were off but it didn't seem to affect the audience response. Sounded like a damn good show, actually.

Matthey felt this completely unreasonable burst of pride. A flush of great, all encompassing maternal pride.

Five minutes later, she was silently calling the cues that ring down the act. As she felt the stage fade to black, the speaker on the wall burst into applause and whistles and cheers. She envisioned the company taking their bows. Soon they'd be running upstairs, this time more ebulliently. Also, more ready to be questioned.

Chuck Lynch stuck his head around the door. "Sir, I thought you'd want to know that Detective Mally is conscious and will be alright. He says that this one here saved his life." He pointed to Matthey. The detective didn't bother to look at her.

"Yes, and?"

"Yeah, they want to know what the hell happened to the corpse? Said he was stabbed, shot, and banged over the head. They figure someone really wanted him dead."

Matthey grimaced.

"Anything else?"

"Yeah, also the girl has finally started to talk. Swears up and down that she didn't do the corpse. Admits cutting Mally but claims the other one did the guy. Headquarters say they believe her."

This time the detective looked at her hard while shouting "get down there fast and make sure that girl doesn't get away. I want to see her now!"

Chapter Twenty-Five

By the time Matthey got downstairs two policemen had Isabel firmly in hand and were leading her out of the building. She presumed they were taking her "downtown for questioning". The girl looked very small between the two burly uniformed cops but she didn't look scared. Isabel glanced back at Matthey just before they went out the stage door. The girl smiled. Matthey shuddered and, in confusion, gave her a thumbs-up gesture. Isabel turned away and Matthey headed for her office.

Both Dr. Tom and Roger were waiting. The therapist sat at the desk and her ex-husband looked very comfortable on the couch sipping from her Bushmills. Sitting on the chair by the door was a man whose age was indeterminate but looked like the years had had enough time to have their way with him. He had a foot-long dirty gray beard and wore an old khaki pair of cut-offs and an orange Grateful Dead tee shirt. A large, very full and carefully knotted trash-bag was on his lap. Before Matthey could say hello, Tony ran in.

"Wow, I think I did O.K. How did it look?"

Matthey sighed. "I have no idea. I sat up in the dressing room the whole time being glowered at by a very hostile cop. It sounded good, though. I'm sure you were great." She looked at the three other men who patiently waited for her attention, all smiling up at her.

"Tony, would you try to find out from someone if we can all go or if they want to question us further or if Alan wants to do notes or what. They've taken Isabel for questioning."

"Sure, do you want me to do the report?"

"Forget it. Everyone was here, anyway. I'll do it tomorrow or next week or never."

Tony smiled at her and left.

What a happy group we all are, Matthey thought. "O.K., guys, things are a little crazy around here as I'm sure you've figured out.

Dr. Tom, I assume you and Roger have met. I hope you enjoyed the show. I'm afraid I'm going to be very busy and can't show you around."

Dr. Tom stood up and gestured toward the bearded gentleman. "Matthey, it is my honour to introduce you to Mr. Clyde Masterson. Once Clyde was an engineer for the Wabash Pacific and now, he is my mentor, my muse, perhaps my soul." Clyde kept smiling at Matthey.

Matthey smiled back, held out her hand and said, "how do you do?"

"By accepting the light and the dark." He took her hand with both of his. "Look at all, close your ears, don't blink. When you succeed at this, you'll have everything you wanted." Clyde dropped her hand and looked modestly away.

Matthey looked at Dr. Tom. Roger sat there drinking the Irish whiskey, smiling his head off.

"Well, Dr. Tom, I see your friend from the plaza was able to join you. That's great." Turning back to the older sage she found him looking in the mirror on the wall across from him. He was attempting to make his earlobes the same length.

"Mr. Masterson, what's your favourite Frankie Laine song?"

"'Granada' brings me eternal joy," said Clyde still looking in the mirror.

"Oh but, 'Moonlight Gambler' is perfection," Dr. Tom shouted.

"Personally," Matthey interjected smugly, "I think 'That Lucky Old Sun' is, by far, the superior cut on that album."

"Perhaps," smiled Clyde.

"At any rate, I hate to be rude but there is just an awful lot of stuff happening around here and I really must ask you all to leave."

165

Clyde stood up, clutching his garbage bag. Dr. Tom gestured him to go through the door first. To do so Matthey had to back out the door and let him by. As Dr. Tom passed by her, he held out his hand to Clyde. Clyde took it and the two men stood clasping hands and smiling at her.

"Matthey, I know I won't be seeing you anymore. I don't think I've failed with you, however. I think I've given you a lot to think about and I'm confident, that with time and the foundation that I've created churning in your life force, that you will come to understand the same truth that I know. When that happens and you want to join with me, know that you will always be welcome. You're always a part of me. Just as Clyde is. Just as all men are."

"And all women."

"Of course. Oh, yes." Still smiling they turned around without dropping hands and walked out the stage door.

Matthey signed and went back in the office, her office, goddammit, to deal with Roger.

"I thought we were going to meet at the Inside Passage." She settled herself into her desk chair.

"Well, yes, I know that's what I said but something came up. Listen, I know you said your shrink was weird, but I can't believe you actually went to that guy for more than one session. That guy's sick."

"Yeah, well, he has his good points. You had to be there. I rather liked Clyde."

"Yeah, well, if you say. Listen, I wanted to tell you something before you heard it from someone else." Roger poured himself another shot. Matthey tensed up slightly.

"There's a woman named Janet Price. I met her a couple of months ago playing volleyball. We went out a bit. Nothing serious, I was married after all, but we had fun and she didn't mind my wife, uh,

Denise. Anyway, last night she told me she was pregnant. She's forty-one and wants the baby. Well, you know how much I want a family and it is my baby, too, and we get along, well, I mean we can laugh together and she says she really loves me and so, uh, she's moved in, is moving in, and, well, I know you really weren't ever going to want to get back with me and probably you're relieved and I hope we can continue to be friends. Actually, Janet's kind of a bit nervous about me seeing you so probably you shouldn't call me at home, but you know I want everything wonderful for you. So, anyway, I just wanted you to know. I'll let you go. Just think, me a father. Wow. I hope I do alright." He stood up.

Matthey also stood up. Her stomach had become a South African ANC fist. Her jaws clenched and she wanted to spit in his face.

"You'll be fine. Congratulations. Wow."

"Yeah, thanks. Well, see you. Bye." Roger threw back the last of his Bushmills and gave her an awkward hug. He smiled at her and disappeared around the corner. She heard the stage door open and close.

Matthey stood there and was surprised when a tear fell from one eye. "Oh, Christ, kiddo, he's right. You didn't really want him. He's entitled to his life. You know it wouldn't have worked out. But, dammit, he gave me the option and now I don't have it. He's going to have a fucking baby and I'm going to have swill. Roger, you fuckin' asshole." She wanted a cigarette. She had stopped smoking ten years ago.

Tony came in. If he noticed her face, he didn't say anything. "The police have taken everyone's name and info. A few people are going down to the station tonight but everyone else is free to go and will be called later. Alan said to send everyone home, no notes. I think he wants time to think what to do about Isabel."

"If she gets booked for killing Che, he won't have anyone in the role tomorrow. Hell, who would want to do it anyway."

"She killed Che!?"

"Well, apparently Gloria admitted gutting Mally but swore Isabel had done Che. That's why they jumped on her as soon as she left the stage."

"Jesus, we have to tell Alan."

"Surely, someone's talked to him. But, yeah, let's go find him and talk to Norman, as well. When I saw them upstairs, they were talking about going to the Inside Passage."

"O.K., I've got to make a couple of phone calls, first."

"Great, let me go up and visit the actors and I'll be back." Matthey headed for the stairs. She yelled good-by to the crew. There was a matinee tomorrow--perhaps--so no rehearsal was scheduled. Upstairs, she let everyone know basically what had developed, omitting the specifics. Said she didn't know about the matinee but to stay by their phones. And if anyone had any great ideas about a new 'Danais' to feel free to make suggestions. Also assured them the show had been terrific and that the 'Shuberts' loved it. They were all in a hurry to leave for the bar and by the time she had visited the last dressing room the other actors and the crew had departed. As she walked downstairs, she realized she really would need to write up a detailed report. She decided to do it at Bill's. And she'd ask Tony to do one as well.

Back in the office Tony was getting his stuff. Lou, the doorman, stuck his head in and asked if he could leave. She said sure and thanked him. He headed out the stage door.

The phone rang just as Matthey was about to lock the office door. "Shit," she muttered as she went back in to answer it.

"Backstage."

"Hello, is Carole there?" a small, tinny voice inquired.

Matthey shuddered and said, "no, I'm sorry she isn't. May I ask who's calling?" At the same time a horrible thought struck her and gestured to Tony to check and see if Carole was still behind the flats. He ran off.

The voice on the other end of the receiver responded, "well, this is her mother. I'm sorry to call you this late but I just came home from the restaurant where I work and there was this message on the machine asking anyone to call. Could you please tell me where she is?"

Tony ran back in. He nodded, grimacing.

Oh fuck, Matthey thought. "Mrs. McDonald, I--"

"Mrs. Fillmore. I remarried after Carole's father left me."

"Mrs. Fillmore, yes, I am very sorry to have to tell you this but...." Matthey listened to herself tell the truth and lie at the same time. Mrs. Fillmore didn't cry. She just asked how she could possibly explain this to Carole's institutionalized, fourteen-year-old daughter. And hung up.

Matthey put down her receiver. "Did Carole ever tell you she had a child?" she asked Tony.

"No."

"Me, neither." Matthey sat back. A grandmother who works nights in a restaurant, her daughter, the mother who's dead and lying forgotten behind some flats in the hall of an empty theatre, and her child waiting in a state home for her mommy. What's the point. This time a tear began to eke out the side of her left eye.

"Let's go to the Inside Passage and when I get there, I'm going to raise hell at the police to get that body out of here. And then I'm going to drink."

Chapter Twenty-Six

Tony and Matthey closed the stage door behind them and made sure it was locked. They headed to the front of the theatre to make their way across the plaza to the restaurant. By now, almost all of the audience had driven off and the grassy square was almost deserted. The fountains were still on, illustrating their dancing waters choreography. A lone figure was sitting on a bench, reflected by the underground lights shining up into the dark night. As they neared the outside ring of water spouts the person stood up. Both Matthey and Tony tensed. It had been that kind of night.

"Matthey," the figure who could now be made out as female said.

She looked familiar to Matthey. Something about the profile in the back lighting. No one from the show, she thought.

"It's Debbie."

Matthey drew in a deep breath. "My God. What are you doing here?" She had walked close enough to make out her face. It looked so young in the shadows and so familiar.

"I was at the show. I've been waiting for you to come out."

"You shouldn't be out here alone." She heard Tony breathing heavily behind her. "Oh, this is Tony, the other stage manager. Tony, this is Debbie, my oldest friend."

The two of them shook hands. Tony excused himself and said he'd go on to the bar. Matthey smiled gratefully at him and asked him to please talk to Norman and Alan and explain she'd be along in a minute. And to call the police about Carole. Tell them you're calling the L.A. Times. He nodded and hurried off.

Matthey looked at Debbie. She was dressed impeccably in a dark blue skirt hitting just at the knee. White blouse with matching blue jacket and a cloth brown coat over her shoulders. Her hair was chin length, un-layered, with bangs. Just as she'd worn it in grade school.

"I guess you're wondering what I'm doing here?"

"It had crossed my mind. Is this your top-secret mission? If I'd known I could have gotten you tickets. Is Ben with you?"

Debbie sat down on the bench again. Matthey shifted a bit to the left so she could continue to see her face.

"No. Ben isn't. Ben and I divorced five years ago. He's living in Akron, Ohio, remarried and managing a rollerskating rink. The kids go to see him two months in the summer and every other Christmas. They look forward to the trip a great deal."

Matthey took her bags off her shoulder and put them on the ground. She sat down next to her oldest friend. She waited for Debbie to continue. When the silence went on longer than was comfortable, she asked, "So Ben asked you to come out here and check on his daughter?"

Debbie looked at Matthey. "No, he didn't. Ben knows nothing about Jacqueline. Jacqueline is my daughter. I gave birth to her seventeen years ago."

Matthey looked at her friend in astonishment and immediately realized she shouldn't. Now she knew why Debbie's silhouette had looked so familiar. It was identical to Isabel. The same tilt of the head, the same stance. Hell, the same damn pert nose now that she really looked.

"What else haven't you told me?"

Debbie put her hands underneath her chin and leaned forward staring into the fountain.

"On spring break of our senior year in high school my parents let me go out to Denver with a friend and her family to ski and look over the university since I would be going there in the fall. The parents pretty much left us alone and since my friend was an expert skier and I wasn't I spent a lot of time on my own. One day, instead of falling down on the bunny slopes, I decided to walk around the campus. I took a bus into town and spent the day exploring the buildings. They were on break as well, but the student union was open, and I stopped in for a soda. I sat down to drink it and read a copy of the student newspaper that was laying there."

"I noticed a boy eating at a table close by. He was older than me and I thought he was gorgeous. He looked foreign and wise. He became aware of me looking at him and asked to join me. I felt very adventurous when I said yes. He asked what I was majoring in and when I said Spanish he told me he was from Cuba and we sat and chatted in Spanish for hours. It was wonderful. He was delightfully flattering. Said he was just finishing up his master's in political history. Anyway, it had started to snow while we were inside and when we got up to leave, we realized it was practically a blizzard outside. He suggested I phone the bus station. It turned out all buses had been cancelled and I ended up calling my hosts and explaining I couldn't get back to the resort that day but would spend the night in a hotel and would return the next day. Well, he invited me to dinner and things progressed and I spent the night with him. It was magnificent. I was a virgin. I've never had a night like that."

Debbie was silent for a minute. Matthey envied her that night.

Debbie continued. "I returned to the mountains the next day and he had my phone number in St. Louis. He was finishing up that June and heading off to parts unknown. I flew back home a few days later, not in love, but exhilarated. Feeling I could do anything. Accomplish whatever I wanted. Several weeks later it dawned on me that I might be pregnant. And, of course, I was. My parents sent me off to stay with an aunt and uncle in Tulsa. I told friends I was going to Europe for the summer and then straight to school. I had the baby in December and started school in January."

Matthey remembered envying that European trip. "What happened to the baby?"

"There was no question, from my parents' end, that the baby would be placed for adoption. I wrote several letters to the address in Denver where'd we spent the night keeping him informed of everything. He never answered but the letters weren't returned. Then a lawyer in Colorado wrote to my aunt and uncle on behalf of a relative of the father's, in Mexico, in Bucerias, that would love to raise the child as their own. My parents agreed and the lawyer arranged everything. A few months later I gave birth and saw my baby for about one minute in a druggy haze. Two weeks later I was back in Denver starting out as a freshman. I'd proficiencied out of several courses and took an extra load and was caught up with the others by the start of the next fall."

"What about the father? Did you see him in Denver?"

"No. He was gone. I've never heard from him again."

Matthey was having some trouble in her thinking. "So, by some bizarre stroke of fate you ran across this letter from the airplane crash and that led to your calling me? How did you know her name was Jacqueline?"

"No, I made all of that up. There was no letter. The stuff I translate is pretty mundane. I wasn't entirely unhappy to give the baby up. I had plans to be somebody. And any real guilt was easily assuaged by knowing that she was with relatives and not total strangers. I assumed she'd at least be acquainted with her father. No, I studied hard and played hard and fell in love with Ben and graduated early and married and became very good at everything I decided to do. I had two children and am a damn good mother. I was a damn good wife, too, but Ben said he got tired of my "perfection", he called it, and when he met this sweet, slightly overweight nurse whose idea of a good time is team bowling, he went for it without looking back. I knew her name was Jacqueline because that was my condition of the adoption. It was the name of my favourite Barbie doll."

"You named your Barbie doll Jacqueline? I didn't know that." Matthey had hated dolls but had condescended to play with them with Debbie.

"It was my secret name for her. You're not supposed to tell anyone. I hated thinking my Barbie was just like everyone else's so I gave her a different name. Every time I'd say Barbie I'd cross my fingers and think Jacqueline."

Matthey stood up. There was a lot to tell Debbie. A lot she didn't know. About Isabel, her child.

"So, what did you think of your daughter's performance? Must have been a surprise seeing her in one of the leading roles."

"She was beautiful. I was in tears the whole time. Will she get to go on again? Is she talented?"

"She is very talented. You must have been shocked by the scar?"

"Not really. They'd written me about her accident."

"Who had written you?"

"After Ben left, I decided I wanted to know what had happened to Jacqueline. My parents still had copies of all the information that had changed hands during the adoption. Through the agency I was able to track down the lawyer who was now living in San Diego. I discovered that a little money can make a big difference in what people remember and decide to tell you. He gave me an address and I wrote assuring them that I only wanted to keep in touch and had no intention of personally seeing the girl. But I did ask them to let me know how she was doing and hoped they'd send me a picture. They, the man and woman who had taken her in, were very kind and wrote me three times over the past four years. The scar was the result of a burn when she was little. An older cousin was pouring hot coffee and she was playing naked underneath him. He lost his balance and poured it all down her back. When I heard she was in the play and I could see her without her knowing it I had to come. Her going on in the lead was a wonderful surprise."

Matthey started pacing. "Wait a minute, Debbie. Was there any truth to anything you told me? How does Che figure in this? Who's he? Does the whole cocaine thing have any validity or was that just some kind of subterfuge? Why is Jacqueline called Isabel?"

"Jacqueline's middle name is Isabel. That's what her adoptive family called her. The green card is legit. I arranged it for her. Without her knowledge, of course. Her adoptive parents told me that Che intended to bring her up to Los Angeles. He was living here, and he intended to help her break into the business. He said she had talent and beauty and he had the connections. He'd always told her how exciting show business was and she always wanted to be in it."

" And I'm assuming that Che is.......?"

"... is her father. Yes. He stayed in touch." Debbie looked at Matthey for the first time and it caused her to glance away. The look was accusatory. "Did you sleep with him, Matthey?"

Sigh. "Yes."

"Well, I can't blame you. He's terrific isn't he. Don't tell me if he wasn't. It's been one of my best memories."

"He was terrific. Listen, Debbie, there's no easy way to say this but Che's dead. He was killed tonight."

Just then the fountains were turned off. The whoosh of the water sinking into the ground almost covered the gutteral choke coming out of the darkness now enveloping the two women.

Matthey decided Debbie had had more in mind with her visit than just seeing her daughter.

"How did it happen? Who did it?"

"So, you just assume someone murdered him, eh? Well, actually, we all did. I mean, I sort of shot him and I sort of stabbed him and it appears that Isabel smashed him over the head." Matthey sat back on the cement bench and took Debbie's hands and gripped them tightly.

"Isabel has been taken to the police station. They think she killed Che, intentionally. They arrested her after the show."

"That's why I didn't see her come out."

"It's a very long story but another actor, a woman, who also has been arrested for stabbing a police officer, is claiming Isabel killed Che. We really don't know."

"Is the other actress named Carole?"

"No, why do you ask?"

"You told Tony to tell the police to take care of Carole."

"No, that's part of the story. Carole's also dead and her body's still backstage. Listen, forget it, it's too much to go into. I imagine you want to help Isabel, uh, Jacqueline?" Matthey stood up and grabbed her bags.

"What's she like, my daughter?"

"Oh," Matthey sighed. "She doesn't speak English that well, so I can't say I really know her. She's, uh, fairly quiet. Tough. Ambitious, I think. Focused. Maybe too many hard edges. In other words, she'll probably go far."

"Do you think she killed him?"

"I don't know. Come on. I have to see Tony, and my director and producer. We'll go in and have a drink and then let's go to your hotel and I'll fill you in on everything."

Debbie stood up and the two of them walked arm-in-arm toward the Inside Passage.

"Did you fall in love with him?"

"No," Matthey answered honestly. "But he sure was gorgeous and he was great in bed!"

"Yeah. Did he do that bit with the grapes?"

"No! What bit? Shit! Was it good?"

"You bet. I'll tell you all about it."

They walked on.

Chapter Twenty-Seven

Matthey walked in the door of Bill's house after two in the morning. Norman and Alan had been apprised of Isabel's situation. A call had gone to George, the casting director. To get someone in soon! One of the other understudies, who was at the bar, volunteered to step in for the role of 'Danais', if necessary. They'd just omit the nudity and cut a few lines. Hardly an ideal solution but the show would go on. Or they might cancel the weekend.

There was some muttering about the role being unlucky. But everyone just had another drink and enjoyed making jokes in poor taste. Alan and Norman were actually in high spirits because of the Shubert's positive reaction. Probably the Quaalude that Alan, undoubtedly, had ingested before the curtain went up didn't hurt either. When Matthey and Debbie left for the hotel, laughter and semi-hysterical cheers were filling the bar. It appeared a fairly festive gathering. Matthey was relieved that no one had been derogatory about Isabel, though she had tried to alleviate the possibility by introducing Debbie as having known the girl.

Back at the hotel they'd talked for two hours. Debbie had switched to club soda after her first wine spritzer and Matthey had decided to follow suit. She was starting to realize that a whole lot of stuff was going on and, perhaps, she should try to understand it. She left Debbie, promising to meet her at the police station at ten the next morning. They'd called and discovered that Isabel was being held but not formally charged. Debbie made some phone calls about getting a lawyer.

As Matthey opened Bill's door, she was surprised to find him still up and sitting in a chair and sober. Both cats were on his lap and the dog was leaning against his legs.

"Hi, what are you still doing up?" She threw her purse and bag on the floor. "I'm sorry I'm so late. Wait till I tell you everything that's been going on."

Well, not everything. Matthey took off her shoes and fell into the couch. Immediately, all three animals shifted over to her.

"Baby, I'm leaving tonight. A limo is on its way to take me to the airport."

179

She looked back at the door and realized there was a suitcase next to it.

Bill continued, "My baby brother called."

That would be Joey. He and Bill hadn't talked in five years. Bill was disgusted with his lack of initiative.

"Joey called to tell me that Jacky has been diagnosed with leukemia and, probably, has only a few months to live."

Jacky was the middle brother. This one Matthey had met. Another lush but a pleasant, benign one. Also, very unambitious. But Bill was close to Jacky.

Matthey was stunned. "My God, Bill, I'm sorry. Can I do anything?"

"Yes, take care of the dog until I can send for her. It shouldn't be long. And feel free to stay here as long as you want. I'll need the mail sent to me for awhile, but I'll soon get it all forwarded. If you can't stay here, I know I'll be able to get one of the kids at work to move in."

"This sounds like you plan to be gone a long time."

"As long as it takes. Jacky doesn't have anyone now that Betts moved out on him, and he needs me. I'll move into his house on Long Island and I'll take care of him. He'd do the same for me."

Matthey doubted that. Maybe his wife, Betts, would have. "I guess this means you and Joe are talking again. That's good."

"That little shit. I don't want anything to do with him, but Jacky likes him. We'll deal with that."

Yeah. "Bill, this is going to be very hard on you. Are you up to it?"

"You mean my drinking. I've been thinking about that. I've never thought it was as bad as you made out. But, for now, I'm stopping. Have stopped. Turns out Jacky's been going to AA meetings back east and I told him we'd do it together. We'll see how it goes." Bill smiled at Matthey. A rueful smile. One with a wealth of unspoken acknowledgement in it.

Matthey smiled back. "That sounds great. I'm sorry about the circumstances but it sounds like this might be a really good thing for all of you in a way. Please give my love to Jacky. I hear all the time about people having remissions."

"Maybe, but the doctors don't think so."

A car pulled into the driveway. The lights flashed through the windows. Bill stood up and looked out.

"That's the limo."

Matthey also stood up and the animals scattered. "I guess I'm not going to see you for a long time. Let me know if I can help...whatever."

"I'll call. I know this hasn't been much of a relationship for you. You've been wonderful. I'll miss you. Find someone you deserve." He put his arms around her and kissed her on the forehead.

"Uh, yeah. I'll miss you, too. I love you, you know."

"I know."

There was a knock on the door. Bill opened it and greeted the driver. The gaunt looking fifty-ish man picked up the suitcase and headed back to the limo. They followed him and waited while he put the suitcase in the trunk and opened up the passenger door.

"I left all the information in an envelope on the kitchen table. I'll call in a couple of days."

"Don't worry about anything here. It'll be fine." She reached to hug him.

This time Bill kissed her on the lips. Not passionately but still there was a hint of the old feelings. Like someone lightly tapping on your door when you're asleep. A fleeting memory that this had once been very good. It seemed so long ago. They walked out to the limo. Bill got in the back seat and the driver shut his door. A few seconds later he drove off into the night. There was just a sliver left of the moon.

Matthey went back into the house and headed for the kitchen. For a beer and for the envelope. She opened it and took out the three sheets of paper. One explained, in a short paragraph, where and why he was leaving. Another had the telephone number and address of his brother. The third listed everything to be taken care of. Vet information, someone to call in the morning and explain Bill's departure. What to say to others who would call. That was it. No letter of any personal nature. If she had returned five minutes later this would have been all she got.

Matthey popped open the bottle of Budweiser and threw a little extra food in the cats' dish. She was angry. She went back to the couch and once again the animals made themselves comfortable on her. She was angry at his lack of sentimentality. She was angry because she didn't get the opportunity to talk to him about her day. She was angry that he was cleaning up his act for his brother and not for her. Yeah, she knew it only worked if he did it for himself, anyway. So, what. Mostly, she was angry at Bill because of the expression on his face as he looked out the limo window at her. It was the face of a man on a mission, a man with a purpose, a meaning. A look that already excluded her and Los Angeles and the industry. Matthey envied him that look. More than she envied Debbie her night in Denver. More than she envied Roger his baby or the group at the Inside Passage their blind optimistic revelry celebrating the Shubert's approval.

God, it hurts when someone in the gutter gets enlightenment and leaves you in the dust. Abandons you while he rides off into the bright lights to seek goodness and integrity. But she always knew he'd hurt her. And she supposed it wasn't as bad as if it had happened a year ago. There was merit in hanging in there. Longer pain but less intense. Hell, they'd just officially broken up a few minutes ago and it was all accomplished very pleasantly. It was now completely over and they both knew it. Oh, a few loose ends to tie up. A few phone calls and then Christmas cards for a couple of years. Then nothing.

Matthey put her beer on the floor and tried to scratch both Cristo's and Gaffer's ears with one hand while stroking Brady's head with the other.

"Well, you guys, it's been quite a night. I've almost forgotten that Che's dead. I've just said good-by to three men in one night, four if you count Dr. Tom. At least the police had promised to remove Carole. Tony had gone back to the theatre to let them in.

Matthey didn't feel like sleeping in the bed alone, so she brought the quilt out to the couch. Gaffer and Cristo settled in around her head and the dog draped himself on top of her feet. Not a lot of room to move but it made her feel very secure. Tomorrow was, after all, another day.

Chapter Twenty-Eight

Monday morning found Matthey driving back from the airport having just shipped Bill's dog to him. He had called her on Sunday saying that he missed Brady too much and wanted him sent. He'd made all the arrangements. Just have him at Delta Airlines by 8:30 the next morning. They had a pleasant, polite conversation about Bill's brother. He was doing fairly well at the moment. Still smoking a lot of grass but off the booze. Bill never touched dope. He appreciated her helping him out. And he gave her the name of two people who'd be happy to house sit. She wished him well. Brady had taken his tranquilizer easily and after fighting the morning rush hour they arrived at the airport where everything went smoothly.

It crossed Matthey's mind on the drive back that she missed Brady as much as she missed Bill. Maybe more.

After getting back to the house she started packing up her stuff. She had maybe two suitcases of clothes and a few bags of books and stage manager supplies. Sunday night, she had called the actor/paralegal subletting her apartment and he agreed he would be out by Monday evening. It had been fine with him. A friend of his had just finished remodeling an extra bedroom in his house and they planned to become roommates anyway. It was no problem to move right away.

The first name on the list Bill gave her said she'd be thrilled to housesit. It would give her a chance to get out from under her mother's thumb. And Bill was one of her absolute favourite people. She was coming over in the afternoon so that Matthey could show her everything. Everything consisted of how to operate the entertainment system and the security system.

Matthey sat on the stool by the phone and looked at her reflection in the mirror over the message table. "I have no idea why I want to move back to that urban claustrophobic thrift store." The construction was still going on behind her apartment. The neighbourhood wasn't great and the paint was peeling but it was hers and that seemed important right now. Bill's nice valley house felt like a tomb. A middle-class, suburban, white-bread Reader's Digest malignancy.

It didn't take long to pack. She wasn't going to drive back over the hills to Hollywood until after the evening rush hour.

So, plenty of time to fix a Monday morning tequila sunrise. And watch something on Netflix. There sure as hell wasn't anything else to do. What a relief, after this weekend.

Debbie had been successful at getting Isabel out of jail. So, she did the Saturday matinee and evening shows and continued to be terrific. Debbie became equally successful at being a stage mother. There was no matinee on Sunday but Alan didn't call a rehearsal, so no further changes happened and there were no notes after the evening performance. So, nothing to do until rehearsal on Tuesday. Matthey doubted there would be much more to the afternoon schedule than a brush-up. Wednesday was opening night and then the show was hers. Alan would leave for Pittsburgh to direct another show. Isabel still had no understudy, but George promised that someone wonderful was coming in Tuesday morning to audition and that it was a sure thing.

Matthey hadn't spent much time with Debbie. She and Isabel chattered away to each other in Spanish and they looked very happy at having found one another. More like two very close sisters than newly introduced mother and daughter. It was strange to see Isabel smiling.

While listening to the blender break up the ice she opened a can of cat food and thrilled Gaffer and Cristo by putting some in their bowls. Just one big happy family in the kitchen. She poured the cold mixture in a glass and threw in a cherry. It was all just a little depressing. God, days off could be dull.

Walking back into the living room she flipped on the TV. Settling back into the couch the two cats jumped up on her and began to groom themselves and each other. The picture on the screen clarified itself as a bedroom set on her soap. Damn, Jill is still fooling that moron.

As Matthey tried to concentrate on the insipid plot gracing the 42-inch illuminated piece of glass in front of her she became aware of a low sound. Almost like an electrical hum. She cocked her head to search for the source of the sound and the couch began to shake. Then she realized the whole room was shaking. The whole house.

"O.K., guys, earthquake!" She jumped up and grabbed the cats and threw them in their cage and ran out the front door. Reaching the middle of the front lawn she stopped and put the cage down. No trees or power lines overhead. She could still feel the ground shake. She saw the neighbours come out of their houses. It was a beautiful day. In the seventies, clear, no smog. She sat down on the lawn and reassured the cats that all was alright.

"I thought you guys were supposed to warn me of this. Don't you have some sixth sense lower brain intuition that clues you into this stuff?"

Just then another tremor hit, same intensity. If they didn't get any worse, it wouldn't be the big one but it seemed wise to hang out a bit. And why not. She had no pressing need to be anywhere. She laid back and did a snow angel in the grass.

Matthey looked up when she heard a car drive into her driveway. A dark, rental car. Debbie and Isabel got out and walked over to her. She didn't get up and they didn't look surprised to see her on the ground. They sat down with her.

"Did you feel the earthquake?" she asked them. One always likes to share earthquakes in California.

"No, we didn't feel a thing." said Debbie. She said something to Isabel in Spanish. The girl shook her head.

"That's too bad we missed it. Guess you don't feel it when you're driving. Gosh, I'd love to have experienced that. Gee, things always happen to you, Matthey."

Matthey smiled. "I suppose they do. Well, what can I do for you guys? Everything alright?"

"Oh, yes, everything's wonderful. My daughter is just perfect. Do you know she's an incredible tennis player? We were just out on the court and she almost beat me."

Debbie spread her flowered rayon skirt out to cover her knees. She took off her white slip-ons with a flower print. Her milky white toenail polish looked newly applied. Isabel was in a sundress that accented her bronze skin and her slim waist. She looked radiant. She also looked nervous. She had newly applied red polish on her toenails.

Debbie cleared her throat and started in. "We've come over here to explain a few things. I'm leaving tonight to go back to Washington. I have to get back to my job. I'll be back out on the weekend. At the end of the run I want Isabel to fly back East and live with me."

Matthey sighed. "I don't mean to sound pessimistic but what about a trial. She's still a major suspect."

"Well, a lot has happened. We've all known Gloria stabbed the police officer. But this morning, she also admitted killing Christine."

"My God." Matthey was truly surprised. They had been so close. Just shows you what I don't know, she thought.

"Apparently, Gloria was involved with Christine's boyfriend. Though he swears they weren't. Anyway, she says he tried to break it off and she flipped out and hotwired the car parked next to Christine's and used it to hit her."

"Pretty chancey. What if Christine hadn't died. She probably could have identified Gloria."

"Well, Gloria is not using all her brain cells. She has a police record of other minor infractions. Mostly disturbances. Anyway, the boyfriend became suspicious but couldn't prove anything. He's the one Gloria had dinner with that night that Isabel went on. He decided to abduct Gloria so she would miss the curtain. There were no guys in a pick-up truck."

"I knew he was a nice guy."

Debbie looked surprised. "What do you mean?"

"He thinks the girl killed the woman he loves, and I know he loved her. Maybe he had an affair, maybe she made a lot out of nothing. I know he adored Christine. He believes Gloria killed her, but he can't prove it or get her to admit it. He knows she's guilty, but he can't bring himself to hurt her. Just tries to wound her career. Which is pretty destructive in this town. But I kinda respect it."

Debbie picked up Isabel's hand and held it in her lap. "He said he hoped it would lead her to blow it. But he thought she'd just scream and yell. Not try to kill anyone. They're not going to charge him with anything. Gloria was with him willingly and all he did was let her out at an inconvenient place. He voluntarily came down to the police station."

"Anything said about Carole?"

"Gloria admitted killing her, too."

"What? Good God, why?"

"She said the girl kept getting in her face. Kept trying to be 'so damn helpful.' She said she did it without really thinking about it. Everyone had gone to dinner and Gloria was waiting for the boyfriend to pick her up. Carole came up and asked if she could do anything for her. Gloria said no and turned to go wait at the front doors and Carole followed and suggested joining her to eat. Gloria dropped some money or something and Carole got down on the floor to pick it up.

189

Gloria said she looked up and saw the weight hanging over the cabinet and she just reached up and gave it a shove. She said she didn't realize she'd killed her. Just meant to shut her up."

Yeah, Carole could be annoying. Kind, helpful, eager and annoying. Shit. Matthey felt her eyes getting wet. She picked some grass and threw it over her jeans, sighing louder than she realized. She remembered dropping acid in college and trying to watch it grow. It did a lot of things in the ten minutes she stared at it, but it did not grow. "What about Isabel? Gloria hasn't confessed to killing Che has she?"

Isabel looked up at the name. She had been very intently staring across the street during her mother's recounting.

"No, Gloria hasn't confessed to that. She, in fact, swears she didn't. But the police don't plan on pressing charges against Isabel. At least not now. It's Gloria's word against Isabel's. And if Gloria accused my daughter it would be easy to convince anyone that she is simply jealous of Isabel's success in the role. Isabel's record is clean."

Matthey could feel Debbie's relief almost as strongly as she felt the earthquake. "I'm sorry to ask this, Debbie, but what do you believe?" She looked at Isabel as she said this. She knew the girl understood.

Debbie didn't hesitate for a second. "I believe in my daughter. I haven't asked her, and I don't know if I will. We've had a chance to do a lot of catching up. Che hadn't been an overly compassionate father. I don't mean he was a brute but Isabel had needs and he was unconcerned. She and I have a chance at a new life together. I intend it to be based on a clean slate. There are a lot of questions she hasn't asked me either." Debbie reached up and touched her child's cheek. Isabel smiled radiantly at her and the two of them stood up.

Matthey looked up at them. The sun was shining behind their heads and Matthey shaded her eyes to see them. She could still see the disappearing crescent moon in the clear sky. "Does Isabel know who followed me that night?"

"The police asked her that. Yes, it was a friend of Che's. Che had taken a fancy to you and wanted to know where you lived and with whom. When you caught on that you were being followed the friend just decided to have fun with you. Teach you a lesson for causing him to feel a fool for being caught so easily."

Isabel was slightly in front of Debbie and as her mother talked there was a slight shadow on her face. Matthey thought she saw the girl's smile broaden. But she could have been squinting.

She heard the phone ring in the house. The machine picked up.

She stood up. "Well, good luck with everything. I guess I'll see you next weekend. See you tomorrow, Isabel."

"I'll be in every weekend. We're going to see an agent now. There's already some interest in Isabel for some project one of the Shubert people are involved in. In a couple of months. And a producer called about a movie.

"It sounds like you're getting quite a line on this business."

"Yes, I bought a couple of books over the weekend. And the lawyer I engaged for Isabel has been helpful. I intend to protect my child."

The phone rang again.

"I'm sure you will. Take care of yourself."

"You, too. You're a good friend, Matthey."

The two of them walked off hand-in-hand to their navy-blue Grand Am. They drove off with a short wave. Matthey sat on the lawn a bit longer. It was a beautiful day. Well, all of the neighbours had gone back inside. She might as well, also. No more shaking of the earth. Picking up the cage, she headed toward the front door.

If the Shuberts have offered Isabel something in a couple of months they're probably not interested in our show. That'll kill Alan and Norman. Well, maybe after the reviews, if they're good, then...oh, who knows. Matthey stopped thinking.

She closed the door behind her, let the cats out of the cage and picked up her drink. Walking into the office, she punched the answer machine for messages.

"This is Detective Mally. Please call me."

Matthey smiled. Bet he doesn't like the way the loose ends have been tied up. Oh well.

The machine beeped again. "Hi, Matthey, this is Frank Tortoni. Jim gave me your name. Hope you get this. I have a show going into rehearsal in Boston in six weeks. It's called <u>A Birthday For Your Nephew, Fran</u> and I need a production stage manager. I have a guarantee that we'll move to Broadway after the four-week run in Boston. If you're interested, please call. A couple of other people already involved in the show have spoken highly about you. My number is....."

Matthey stood there listening to the telephone number. She took a sip. She smiled.

THE END

ACKNOWLEDGEMENTS

I am grateful to every play, musical, benefit, industrial, reading I have ever done in theatre around the United States, Japan, and Canada. I am grateful for the wealth of experiences I have had from Broadway to regional to summer stock to 99-seat waiver, and so much more. I've been fortunate to work with top directors, designers, actors, producers, playwrights, technicians, administrators and every other artist that is part of the creative process called theater. I've worked with a lot of not so top folks as well. And that makes for a lot of stories to tell my stage management class and to write about.

I want to thank the stage managers that I've worked with who always taught me how to be better. You know who you are.

I want to thank friends and colleagues who understand that none of this is truly based upon them or anyone or anything they know but it's easier to take some flavor from personal experiences. And it's fun.

And I want to thank my family – my husband, Paul Perri, who always reminds me I can be a better person, and my children, Jake and Justine, who fill my soul with wonder. And my sister, Dixie, who has had my back since I was born. And I want to thank my brothers and my nieces and nephews and my dear friend, Cathy, who have always challenged me to do better, even if they don't realize it.

CPSIA information can be obtained
at www.ICGtesting.com
Printed in the USA
FSHW022341071121
86042FS